"You're all

Jake called to Patience in the kitchen.

Diving headfirst from the doorway, Patience blindsided him with a massive tackle. She was strong. And fit. But Jake knew she thought of him as a New Yorker who wasn't up to a good fight with a woman who could fell trees and build fires.

But she'd underestimated him.

She glanced up at him, and in her eyes he saw she was aware of her mistake.

"Don't you dare," she said.

He laughed. "Too late."

Her sweater had gotten scrunched up under her breasts, exposing a tempting expanse of bare midriff, and how could he have resisted?

"Now for my revenge," he murmured.

Carla Neggers has always had a love/hate relationship with New York City. So she had a lot of fun creating a nature-loving heroine who is out of her element in the big city. Like the heroine in *Trying Patience,* Carla comes from a close-knit—"and some would say eccentric"—family. She currently lives in the mountains of Vermont with her husband and two children.

Books by Carla Neggers

HARLEQUIN TEMPTATION

Don't miss any of our special offers. Write to us at the following address for information on our newest releases.

Harlequin Reader Service
P.O. Box 1397, Buffalo, NY 14240
Canadian address: P.O. Box 603,
Fort Erie, Ont. L2A 5X3

TRYING PATIENCE

CARLA NEGGERS

Harlequin Books

TORONTO • NEW YORK • LONDON
AMSTERDAM • PARIS • SYDNEY • HAMBURG
STOCKHOLM • ATHENS • TOKYO • MILAN
MADRID • WARSAW • BUDAPEST • AUCKLAND

Published January 1993

ISBN 0-373-25527-6

TRYING PATIENCE

1

"PATIENCE MADRID, you're becoming a hermit just like Uncle Isaiah."

Taking no offense at Tilly's comment, Patience stretched out on her ratty couch. Contrary to her sister's opinion, she lived comfortably in her two-room log cabin that was situated on a quiet, crystal lake in the southern Adirondack Mountains. Patience pictured her sister on the phone in her elegant condo overlooking Central Park. From her tone, Patience could guess her older sister was already exasperated with her. "The answer is still no."

"Oh, come on, do me a favor. A couple weeks in the city will do you good."

Tilly was nothing if not stubborn. Patience said calmly, "I hate the city."

"You're just saying that to annoy me. You know, Patience, pretty soon you won't know how to talk to anybody but that confounded dog of yours."

"'Confounded'? That must be city talk. Back in the old days, you'd at least have said damned dog."

Tilly sniffed. "That was before Terrence."

Indeed. Scholarships to Smith and Yale and ten years working on Wall Street hadn't changed her sister, but marriage to Terrence Terwilliger and life on Central Park West certainly had. She even called herself Matilda these days. Said Tilly Terwilliger sounded ridiculous. Patience thought it was impossible to avoid sounding ridiculous with Terwilliger as a last name, but that wasn't her problem: *she* wasn't married to Terrence.

Her sister resumed her argument. "Apollo and Aphrodite are lovely cats."

"I hope they didn't hear you. I've never met a Persian that likes to be called something as ordinary as a cat. Especially your two. Me, I like a good mouser."

Tilly sighed in a ladylike manner. Ladylike sighs were one of the oddities that life among the Terwilligers had taught her. Right now her older sister would be perched on a white chaise longue, dressed delicately in a white satin robe, fingernails and toenails painted. She'd be wearing makeup, expertly applied, and have her hair up, neat and sophisticated. Patience—four inches taller than Tilly, bigger boned, leaner—had on her black trail pants and white fleece pullover she'd worn on her evening trek around the lake with her dog, Jake.

Tilly had said daffodils were blooming in New York City. They weren't blooming in the mountains—the ice was barely melted off the lake.

"You haven't been to New York in ages." The Terwilliger influence hadn't managed to break Tilly's spirit when it came to a fight. "Think of all the fun you could have. I could set up an appointment for you with my hairdresser—"

"For what?"

"For that mop of yours, that's what."

Patience grinned. Matilda Terwilliger was sounding more like the old Tilly Madrid. Even before Terrence, she'd threatened to make an appointment with her hotshot New York hairdresser to tackle her younger sister's long, wild, frizzy red hair. At two hundred dollars a cut, Patience preferred to stick to trimming her own hair with their late Uncle Isaiah's old barber scissors. Tilly said it looked like it.

"Okay, okay, you win." Tilly sounded frustrated, which she probably was. "Forget I even asked. If you don't want to look after Apollo and Aphrodite for me, I won't make you. I can take a hint."

Patience hadn't been hinting—she'd been out-and-out refusing to cat-sit for her sister.

She sat up, suddenly hearing the wind howling on the lake. It was a familiar sound, sometimes comforting, sometimes downright eerie. Right now it made her feel peculiarly alone. Had her sister's words gotten to her?

"What would I do with Jake?" she asked.

"Jake?"

As if she didn't know. "My dog, Tilly. Can I bring him?"

"No!" Tilly sounded as if she'd nearly choked. "Patience, no, you can't even *think* about bringing that animal to New York. Our neighbors . . ." She trailed off, leaving Patience to imagine what the neighbors would think. Obviously nothing good. "Jake wouldn't be happy here. He wouldn't fit in."

Patience looked down at Jake. Apparently unaware of his enormous size, he'd squirmed as far as he could under the old-fashioned kitchen wood stove. She didn't know why he didn't burn up. And he looked foolish, which wasn't difficult with his looks. He was a scraggly mutt of no particular charm or beauty. As near as she could figure, he was part black Lab, part German shepherd, with maybe a touch of rottweiler. He'd wandered out to the cabin last spring—a scrawny, parasite-infested, lovable, abandoned puppy. His most endearing trait was a love of canoeing equal to Patience's own. He'd even learned, if the hard way, not to leap out in the middle of the lake. After a few near drownings, he'd managed to cure himself of that particular bit of idiocy. The dog wasn't smart.

"Jake's just an ordinary dog."

"He is *not* an ordinary dog, even by country standards. By city standards—Patience, trust me. It would be a serious mistake to bring him."

"He likes cats."

Tilly was silent. She didn't hiss or curse the way she would have before she'd married Terrence and his Terwilliger trust fund a year ago. She'd even stopped arguing politics. She and Patience and Uncle Isaiah and whatever other Madrids happened to be around used to argue politics all the time, even when they agreed. Now Tilly believed in avoiding subjects likely to cause fights among her guests. What was a party for?

"If I can't bring Jake," Patience went on, a stubborn woman herself, "I can't come."

"Patience..."

There was something in Tilly's voice that hadn't been there before. A tentativeness, even a note of un-Madridlike desperation. Patience got up and walked slowly across Uncle Isaiah's old hand-braided rug to her wood stove, her main source of heat. "Tilly, is something wrong?"

"No, of course not. I mean—" She broke off, uncharacteristically inarticulate. "It's just that I need to get away. I need to relax. And I can't if I'm worried about the cats. You know they hate the kennel."

"What does Terrence say?"

"He says they're my cats," Tilly answered, with a touch of the sharpness that had long been a Madrid trait. It didn't take a great leap of imagination to figure out that Terrence wasn't as fond of Tilly's cats as Tilly herself was.

"Til?"

"Please come."

"Til, are you and Terrence on the skids?"

Not a sound from the New York end of the line.

"He *is* going on this trip with you, isn't he?"

Tilly made a small, pained sound that wasn't like her at all. She was always so confident, so optimistic. "He's going on a trip, but not with me."

Patience kept her initial response—which was un-
kind, to say the least—to herself. She could read between the lines. Still, she didn't want Tilly to know
she'd developed her own suspicions about Terrence
Terwilliger III. The man had too much money and had
lived in New York too long to be trusted.

"Business?" Patience asked, feigning innocent curiosity.

"He—Terrence needs to get away, too. We agreed
to go off alone on—I don't know what you'd call it—
a personal retreat, I suppose. I'm going to Arizona,
he's going to Florida."

"Ouch."

Patience rummaged in the woodbox, not prepared
to counsel anyone—even her one and only sister—on
matters of the heart. And at Tilly's wedding last year,
she'd vowed to mind her own business and stay out
of her sister's love life.

"We hope this will be a positive step in our relationship," Tilly said, sounding as if she was quoting
her husband, who tended to talk like that. "He
would...well, Patience, you know how Terrence feels
about your dog."

The first time Terrence Terwilliger III had ventured
out to her spot on the mountain lake, Jake had pinned
him in his fancy white Jaguar. Jake did look mean and
he had a ferocious bark, and although Patience tried
to keep him groomed, some things were hopeless.
Still, beyond deterrence, he was useless as a guard
dog. She'd told Terrence that. "Ter," she'd said, cer-

tain she was the only person who'd ever called him that, "Jake wouldn't hurt anything, not even you." He hadn't been reassured. Her brother-in-law, Patience had come to realize, didn't entirely trust her.

"He thinks Jake has fleas," Tilly said.

"I'm insulted."

"And worse."

"I didn't think Terrence was capable of imagining anything worse than fleas."

"He is a bit of a stuffed shirt," Tilly agreed.

"You sure he'll let me tend your precious Persians? How does he know I won't have them stuffed while you two are off on your separate 'retreats'?"

"He knows you're a soft touch for animals. It's men you'd have stuffed."

"Hey, we're discussing your love life, not mine."

"Not that there's a whole lot to discuss," Tilly commented, clearly unable to resist.

Patience wasn't offended. Tilly actually was being kind: there wasn't *anything* to discuss regarding Patience's nonexistent love life, not since she'd broken up eighteen months ago with the geology professor whose idea of a romantic date was collecting rock samples from lake bottoms.

Her tone softened. "You really need to get away, don't you, Til?"

"Yes, and Terrence does, too. We agreed to go off at the same time, to work separately on certain issues in our marriage so that we can better work on them together when we return to New York."

Patience couldn't imagine. During her thirty-two years, she'd had a few of what could be referred to as relationships and she'd always preferred to hash things out up close and personal, right then and there, while she was still piping hot. Which was maybe why her sister had just accused her of being a hermit and there wasn't currently—nor was there likely soon to be—a man of any romantic import in her life.

"So, you'll come?" Tilly asked, not quite pleading. She still had her Madrid pride.

Lifting the grate on her wood stove, Patience shoved a chunk of wood onto the dying fire. She had to be out of her mind. During her last visit to New York, she'd developed a sinus infection from the polluted air. And a cabdriver had screamed at her, when she'd blithely opened her door into oncoming traffic, "Lady, if you want to get yourself killed, not on my meter, okay?" She didn't like New York. She liked her lakeside cabin in the Adirondacks where it was just her and Jake and the occasional stray critter. Give her a lost moose any day over a bunch of dirty pigeons in Central Park. Not to mention the Terrence Terwilligers of the Big Apple.

But she heard herself say, if without enthusiasm, "Yeah, I'll come."

"I'll arrange for a plane ticket—"

"Nope. I'll drive."

Tilly hesitated. "Patience..."

"Don't start on my Jeep next. You want your kitty-cats looked after by family, family is what you get."

LITTLE THINGS had conspired against Jake Putnam
Farr, and instead of climbing tall peaks in a warm cli-
mate, he found himself standing in an apartment
covered with drop cloths and plaster dust. Men in
coveralls moved busily around him. Electric tools
buzzed and whined. The unfortunate thing was, the
chaos was Jake's apartment. He'd occupied the spacious co-op apartment in a corner building on Manhattan's Upper West Side for the past decade, but only
recently had he let an architect friend talk him into
knocking down a wall or two and generally sprucing
the place up. "We'll retain the twenties ambience,"
Franco had said. He could have said turn-of-the-
century flavor and Jake would have believed him for
all the attention he paid to such things. In fact, he'd
planned to be out of town for the duration of the renovations. But if Jake thought he was in the wrong
place at the wrong time, his friend Terrence Terwilliger looked distinctly out of his element amidst the
chaos.

"I'm sorry your trip fell through," Terrence said.

"Me, too. March isn't one of New York's finer
months."

A carpenter, carrying a sloshing bucket of some sort
of white glop, pushed past Terrence with an irritable
grunt. A fat, oozing gob of the stuff just missed splat-
tering onto the knife-creased leg of Terrence's cus-
tom-tailored suit. "What're you going to do?" asked
Terrence. "Obviously you can't stay here."

Jake shrugged. "I suppose I'll just have to roll out my sleeping bag and camp out on the living room floor—provided there is one. Franco said he'd have made allowances if he'd known I'd be around."

"I'm sure," Terrence said dubiously. He was a man unaccustomed to making do with anything more onerous than a double instead of a king-size bed. At thirty-seven, he was whip-lean, tall, fair, and good-looking in a boyish way—he had dimples women tended to think were adorable. In short, he was the exact opposite of the kind of man people expected would be Jake Putnam Farr's best friend. Jake himself wasn't fair and he wasn't that tall—a couple of inches under six feet—and nobody had ever called him adorable.

"What about Westchester?" Terrence suggested.

Jake's parents resided in Westchester. So did his older brother and sister. He shook his head. "I'd rather hang a hammock from the rafters. I still haven't recovered from Christmas. Mother had an open house and invited every fair-haired damsel within miles. Father grilled me on whether my mountain-climbing was distracting me from business. Lisa introduced me to all her single and divorced friends and kept thrusting babies onto my lap, presumably to show me what I was missing by not being a father. I still haven't managed to get the spit-up stains out of my favorite sweater. And Jeffrey offered to hunt up debutantes young enough to be my daughter."

Terrence laughed. "Serves you right for remaining one of New York's most eligible bachelors. They just want to see you happy and settled—"

"I *am* happy and settled." A change of subject was in order. "When are you and Matilda leaving on your trip?"

"Tomorrow evening at some ungodly hour. Matilda prefers to travel late in the day. In fact, she suggested that if you want to stay at our place you're perfectly welcome. I think it's a wonderful idea."

"It's nice of you to offer, but if I have to cat-sit—"

"Oh, no. Matilda's arranged for the cats to be boarded in the country while we're out of town."

Terrence said "the" cats rather than "her" cats because of his discreet gentlemanly manner. But Jake knew damned well they were Matilda's cats. He had caught Terrence angrily muttering to himself while he picked their long white hairs off his trousers. Terrence adored his wife, however, and had learned to tolerate her cats. Jake, who preferred his animals wild, couldn't stand them.

"I know you're not terribly fond of cats," Terrence added.

"I hate cats," Jake said.

"They're not so bad once you get used to them."

"Domesticated animals don't appeal to me. I don't even like dogs. The last animal I enjoyed up close was a trout I caught on the Batten Kill. I grilled him over an open fire."

Terrence smiled. "Matilda says you're all bark and no bite. But if you'd like to stay at our place, you won't have to worry about the cats or animals of any kind. Look, Jake, it's not just the renovations. You're bored. A change of scenery would do you good."

"Bored? Where the hell'd you get that idea?" But Jake already knew. "Matilda."

Terrence neither confirmed nor denied.

"Well, she's wrong. Just because I've advanced my business to the point where my people don't need me breathing down their necks every day, just because I have *time* now to do the things I enjoy—like fly-fishing and mountain-climbing—doesn't mean I'm bored."

"So I've told her."

A carpenter grumpily asked Jake to move aside so he could get by with his stepladder. "I could always pack up and go to a hotel," Jake said, half to himself.

"What for?"

Terrence wasn't one to part with a nickel if he didn't have to. It was a trait that had annoyed every woman in his life until Matilda Madrid, whose attitude toward money was purely pragmatic. And who clearly loved her husband for who he was, not for what she could get out of him.

"To be honest, Jake," Terrence went on, "you'd be doing us a favor if you stayed at our place. We haven't been gone for more than a weekend at a time since we bought it, and we don't have anyone to look after it. I believe our building's quite secure, but I'd rather not find out the hard way. And since Matilda's taken care of the cats, I think you'd enjoy yourself."

The Terwilligers' new apartment on Central Park West, Jake had to admit, was tough to resist. Spacious and beautifully decorated, with incredible views of the park and the city, it also managed to remain very livable. Matilda's doing.

In contrast, Terrence had grown up on a Westchester estate that might have come out of an F. Scott Fitzgerald novel. When he was growing up, kids used to say Buckingham Palace would seem informal to a Terwilliger. In comparison to Terrence's family, Jake's parents were paupers. But Matilda's past remained something of a mystery. Terrence didn't talk much about where he'd found Matilda, nor about her family and the ultraprivate wedding, which, rumor had it, had taken place on a mountain lake up north. Jake had been off scaling peaks in New Zealand at the time. He'd have flown back, but Terrence had urged him not to bother—he and Matilda wanted a quiet wedding. Jake could guess why. He'd heard—not from Terrence—that the Madrid family were an odd bunch. Supposedly there was an uncle who'd been a hermit and a sister who'd once brought home a wounded moose calf—or whatever the devil baby moose were called—with the idea of nursing the creature back to health. Jake took most of the talk with a grain of salt. There was no more normal or sweet a woman than Matilda Madrid Terwilliger.

The carpenter with the bucket of white glop came at them again and rather rudely suggested they remove themselves to the kitchen. Jake was persona non grata in his own apartment.

He relented to his friend's offer.

Terrence beamed, digging out his house keys. "Terrific. I'll inform the doormen. I know you'll have a great time."

Jake accepted the keys, then stopped his friend halfway to the foyer. "You and Matilda have a good trip."

"Thank you. I'm sure we will."

"You'll leave phone numbers?"

"Of course."

"Terrence . . . everything's okay, isn't it?"

"What?" He seemed surprised by the question. "We're taking our first trip since our honeymoon—what could possibly be wrong?"

Jake had no answer. For a few weeks now, he'd sensed a preoccupation on Matilda's part, a tension that hadn't existed before. It could have been adjusting to life among the Terwilligers. Decorating their new apartment. Giving up her job on Wall Street, which, she insisted, had been totally her idea. Jake didn't know. And he doubted Terrence would tell him. In their long friendship, they'd never intruded in each other's romantic life. If Terrence wanted to talk about any problems he and Matilda were having, he would. But he never had before. One reason could be that Jake Putnam Farr, black sheep of his own family, wasn't the best person to give advice about marriage. Jake considered himself a loner. He did his best work alone. He enjoyed mountain-climbing best when alone. And although he didn't always sleep alone, he had always lived alone. He wasn't about to let the potential troubles of the pretty red-haired wife of his best friend—a woman who liked cats—upset his life. If nothing else, Matilda's troubles were none of his business.

"Enjoy your stay," Terrence said. "I'll send you a postcard from Florida."

"Have fun."

Terrence smiled. "Oh, I will."

"And give Matilda my best."

But Terrence was already out the door.

A few minute later, so was Jake, when a man with a monstrous crowbar asked him if he planned to hang around all day. Central Park West would have to be an improvement, especially if Matilda had shuffled her Persians off to the country. He really didn't care for cats.

PATIENCE ROSE EARLY on the morning she was to leave for New York—a very chilly, but beautifully clear, Saturday. She pulled on jeans, a turtleneck and the Norwegian wool sweater she'd had since college, jumped into a pair of mud boots, called her dog and headed down to the lake. It was a short walk from her cabin. She didn't have anything that resembled a lawn: no Kentucky bluegrass, no trimmed shrubs, no neat perennial borders. What she had were evergreens and oaks and maples and lots of scraggly bushes most people would poison if they found them in their yards. She and her sister had inherited the

cabin and thirty-acre parcel from their Uncle Isaiah.
He'd used it as a hunting cabin before retiring there for
the last years of his life, when he'd become something
of a hermit. Patience had cleared out most of the junk
he'd left behind, including a stuffed moose head. She
wasn't a hunter herself, but hadn't gotten rid of the
thing on account of any serious objection to the prac-
tice. She'd simply caught herself talking to the
damned moose once too often.

Jake walked out with her to the end of the small
dock, where the early morning fog still swirled over
the quiet lake. There were four other cabins on its
shores; hers was the only one that had been winter-
ized. Town, such as it was, was a relatively easy six-
mile drive. Her nearest year-round neighbor was a
little more than two miles off. She couldn't even guess
how far it was to the nearest mall or department store.

The air smelled of pine and damp earth, and she
took in deep lungfuls of it, knowing New York
wouldn't be as conducive to deep breathing.

"Well, Jake, what d'you think?" She wondered if
talking to a dog was much better than talking to a
stuffed moose head. At least Jake was alive. "I'm giving all this up for a couple of weeks in a fancy New
York apartment with two fancy New York cats."

Jake rolled onto his back, paws in the air. A friend
down in Lake George had agreed to take him in her
kennel. Jake had never stayed in a kennel before.

"You'll be a good dog, won't you, Jake?"

He flopped his legs back down onto the dock,
coming perilously close to the edge as he rolled onto

his side. He wasn't much for water. Those few times he'd leaped from her canoe had been the result of his low IQ, not any desire for a swim. Occasionally Patience could get him in for a morning dip alongside her, but generally he preferred to bark at her from shore.

"You'd hate New York more than a kennel."

But he'd never been to New York. Jake was a sociable dog. What if he liked it? He snapped lazily at something. Knowing Jake, Patience assumed it was just thin air. She'd brushed him for his trip to the kennel. He still looked scraggly and a lot meaner than he was. He just wasn't a neat dog. But, no matter what Terrence Terwilliger III claimed, he didn't have fleas, and it was no small task keeping a country dog free of parasites.

Terrence and Tilly had left on their separate vacations last night. In a rare concession, her sister had allowed that Apollo and Aphrodite would manage on their own for the night. "But get here as soon as you can tomorrow morning," she'd said in a final, quick call to Patience. "And don't bring that dog of yours!"

Of course, Tilly was at that very moment in Scottsdale, Arizona. She'd never know if Patience had snuck Jake into her apartment.

Jake laid his head on her foot. "If I took you to New York," she said, "you'd behave yourself, wouldn't you?"

He would. She knew he would. How much trouble could a dog like Jake get into?

She rousted him up and headed back to the cabin. To spiff him up for the ride to the city, she tied a red bandanna around his neck. If it lasted until the interstate, she'd be surprised. But he did look a bit less ferocious.

"Come on, Jake."

He followed her outside and off the porch to her old Jeep, hopping automatically into the front seat beside her. The stupid dog did love to ride.

Patience patted him on the head. "You big ugly thing, you. Well, my friend, we're off to the big city."

2

SIX HOURS LATER, Patience pulled into Tilly's parking garage amidst the noise, pollution and tall buildings of Manhattan's Upper West Side. The attendant started to make a crack about her Jeep. Then he saw Jake and turned polite. When Patience mentioned the Terwilligers, he straightened up and turned outright gracious. She wasn't sure she liked that. In her world-view, good manners should stem from values and principles, not power and social position. She was about to launch into a discussion of this conviction when the attendant asked her to get out of her Jeep and give him the key. As she did so, Jake leaped out behind her. The attendant backed up a few steps.

"He's harmless," Patience said.

Behind her, a lady jumped back into her Mercedes-Benz. Jake's booming bark echoed in the parking garage. The woman rolled up her window.

New Yorkers, Patience thought as she finished up her business with the nervous attendant, then headed out to the street with Jake loping at her side. He'd never worn a leash, as far as she could recall. Not that he was well-trained—he just didn't need one out by the lake.

"Heel," she said, just in case he would.

Fortunately, New York was a strange enough place, and Jake did hold a fundamental respect for cars. He stayed at her side. They walked over to Central Park West, as dramatic and busy a street as Patience remembered from her previous brief visits. She loved the American Museum of Natural History at West 79th Street. Tilly's building was within easy walking distance. And Zabar's, a one-of-a-kind deli on Broadway, wasn't that far, either. She and Jake'd manage a couple of weeks in town.

At the entrance to Tilly's building, with its elegant green awning, one of the uniformed doormen opened the door of gleaming glass and polished brass, and didn't object when Jake streaked in ahead of Patience. She'd tied his bandanna back around his neck and he looked quite dapper.

"Heel," she said again, this time to alleviate any fears in people nearby that Jake might not be an obedient New York dog.

"May I help you?" the doorman asked.

"I'm Patience Madrid." At his blank look, she quickly amended, "Matilda Terwilliger's sister."

"Of course. Mrs. Terwilliger left her key for you. Just a moment, please."

He went into a small office adjoining the lobby, which was an impressive place of mirrors, brass, shining wood paneling and porcelain urns of fresh-cut flowers. The Oriental rug would have covered her cabin floor twice. Maybe more. Tilly was a lucky woman, Patience thought; she was living the life she wanted to live. But so was her younger sister. More or less. As much as Patience enjoyed her solitary life in the Adirondacks, she wouldn't have minded having a couple of kids, but that necessitated men and romance, and if there was anything she didn't understand, it was men and romance. Better off just to stick with Jake for company.

She'd almost forgotten him.

"Jake," she called softly.

He was gone. Just like that. There was no sign of him—he hadn't even made a sound. He'd just vanished. Now she'd have to hunt him down and maybe get in trouble with the doormen her first day in town. They'd notify Tilly about her sister's monstrous, undisciplined dog, and Tilly would be furious.

"Jake," Patience said, a little louder.

He didn't come. He never did when she called, unless he really wanted to. She didn't even have a good steak bone on her. It just wasn't the sort of thing one brought to elegant Central Park West.

The doorman handed her an envelope with Tilly's keys inside. "Here you go, Miss Madrid."

She smiled so he wouldn't think anything was up. "Thank you."

Tilly had included a terse note: "Thanks—have a great time in the city! And you damned well better have left that dog home. Til."

Not five minutes in her sister's building and Jake had already gone off solo. This, Patience thought, did not portend well for her stay in the city.

She crumpled up the note, which, at least, had sounded like the Tilly of old.

Behind her, the doorman yelled, "The flowers!"

Whirling around, Patience saw Jake bounding out from under an antique-looking table. The doorman steadied a teetering urn of flowers before it could topple over. His eyes cut over to Patience.

"Jake's forever squeezing into places where he just doesn't fit," she explained.

The doorman didn't comment.

Jake trotted up to her. "You old rascal," she said. Given the mischief he could have created, she was rather relieved. She reached down to grab his collar, if only to mollify the still panicky-looking doorman. No doubt sensing he was about to be marched off like a recalcitrant toddler, Jake shot past her, slipping on the Oriental carpet, sliding on the polished floor, hellbent for who knew what or where.

"Miss," the doorman said, quiet but firm. "Your dog."

As if she didn't have eyes. *"Jake!"*

It was a full-blown country yell, but Jake ignored her.

Patience could see Tilly's reputation with the doormen and possibly her entire building in permanent ruin. *"Mrs. Terwilliger, about your sister and her dog . . ."*

Terrence would never understand.

Jake was heading toward the elevator when its brass doors suddenly opened. Patience hoped this was her chance. Jake had never seen an elevator before. He'd be scared and curious. He'd slow down.

She lunged toward him.

Without so much as a split second's hesitation, he skidded through the parted elevator doors.

"Jake, you rotten *beast!*" Patience yelled, with no effort to citify her voice.

Then she groaned.

A man—a dark, well-dressed, unamused-looking man—glared out at her from within the elevator.

Completely hyper by now, Jake jumped up on the poor guy and placed two enormous paws on his chest, pressing him against the elevator's far wall, panting into his face. Patience imagined saliva, dog's breath. She had to do something.

But the elevator doors began to close silently, and even as she broke into a run across the carpet, wrinkled and askew from Jake's mad dash across it, she knew she'd never get there in time.

Just before the doors shut with a delicate thud, she saw a thatch of wild dark hair and two wild dark eyes—human eyes, not dog eyes—pinned on her.

"Oh, dear."

Patience watched, impotent, as the floor lights above the elevator flicked on one by one, Jake and his companion ascending to parts unknown of her sister's ritzy building.

The doorman came up behind her. "Miss Madrid—"

She turned, smiling her amiable best, attempting to reassure. "Jake's really very friendly."

The doorman's stern look softened; he seemed almost relieved. "Oh—well, thank heaven you know him."

Patience frowned. Of course she knew him. He was her dog. It wasn't as if she'd tried to deny it. But maybe she *should* disown the incorrigible mutt. Pretend she'd never seen him before. About-face, walk out of the fancy lobby with what shreds of dignity she had intact and never return.

Except then Tilly would come home to a couple of starved Persians. And Jake? Well, she couldn't leave an entire building of cowardly New Yorkers to her dog.

Squinting up at the floor lights, she saw that the elevator had stopped at the fourteenth floor. That was Tilly's floor. Now it was on its way back down.

What if Jake had panicked and mauled the man?

Nah. It'd never happen. Whatever else Jake was, he wasn't violent. At home he'd lie on the front porch and practically let rabbits and squirrels run over him.

But this was New York. . . .

The elevator came straight down to the lobby. The doors parted, and there was Jake, sitting with his tongue wagging. But for his crooked bandanna, he was the model of an obedient dog.

There was no dark-haired, dark-eyed man.

"What'd you do, Jake," Patience muttered, blocking off any escape and jumping into the elevator with him, "eat the poor guy?"

Not everyone loved dogs. Terrence Terwilliger, for example. Hated dogs. *Really* hated her dog. Tilly used to love dogs, but now she loved cats. Expensive cats.

The doorman peeked uneasily into the elevator. "Where's Jake?"

Assuming she was blocking his view, Patience moved aside as she pressed the button for floor fourteen. "Right here."

The doorman's face went quite pale. Before she could ask him what was wrong, the doors shut and the elevator whisked her and Jake upward.

She collapsed against the elevator wall. "That was a hell of an entrance, Jake," she sighed. At least the worst was over. She'd get Jake safely into Tilly's apartment, buy a leash and avoid every dark-haired, dark-eyed man in the building. In the whole damned city, if she had to.

She'd also probably have to bribe the doormen to keep them quiet about Jake. The last thing she needed—and Tilly, too, she'd guess—was to have him squealing to Terrence and getting him all upset about Tilly's weird family. It might further strain their marriage, and Patience wasn't supposed to aggravate the situation. She wanted to help.

Jake was panting hard.

"I have no sympathy," she told him sternly. "Clearly, Jake, you just can't be trusted."

But he looked at her innocently, and she couldn't
help it, she just had to laugh. After that episode, the
rest of her visit to New York would be anticlimactic.

Unless she ran into the man from the elevator again.
But it was a big building. How likely, really, she
thought, was that to happen?

JAKE FARR FIGURED he was lucky to have escaped the
elevator with all important body parts intact.

Catching his breath in the Terwilligers' apartment,
he then changed into a fresh shirt. The damned dog
had soiled his favorite shirt with his muddy paws and
spit. It was magenta canvas with black buttons and a
good fit. If the hairy, slobbering mutt had an owner
who could be found, Jake would consider demanding a new shirt. Hell, he'd sue for damages. How much
could he get for being trapped in an elevator with an
unruly stray? He hadn't actually been *hurt*, but what
about mental suffering? It was irresponsible to let such
a creature run around loose.

How the hell had the monster gotten past the doormen?

Jake grunted. *In his place, would you have tried to
stop him?* he asked himself.

Tucking in a fresh, deep blue cotton shirt that didn't
have black buttons, he wondered if he should phone
downstairs, just in case the doormen didn't know
about the slobbering beast running amok in the
building. Jake had debated trying to get the dog to
follow him into the hall. On their mad ride upward,

he'd held steady, managing to creep one hand along the wall of the elevator and press the button to the fourteenth floor. The mutt had collapsed onto Jake's feet. But out in the hall, in safety, Jake had no trouble resisting the temptation to be noble. The dog had shown no sign of wanting to budge, and Jake hadn't been of a mind to insist.

Just as well that Terrence and Matilda were out of town. They'd only left last night and already all hell was breaking loose. Jake could imagine Terrence's reaction to being locked up in an elevator with a salivating dog.

But never mind the damned beast, Jake thought. What about the woman?

He could still see her mass of strawberry hair and hear her yell, *"Jake, you rotten beast!"*

Usually he at least recognized people who held such a low opinion of him. She couldn't have been a recent date. Surely he'd have remembered. The sister or friend of a recent date? But he doubted it. He wasn't known for treating women badly.

There was, however, the ghost of something familiar about her. A client? No way. Though he'd learned to delegate much day-to-day work to his staff, he knew his clients, and none would call him a rotten beast, at least not to his face.

An associate or competitor or employee of a client?

Someone who clearly knew his name and clearly had a bone to pick with him. And knew where to find him, unless that had just been a coincidence.

Now that he'd survived his ordeal with the dog, Jake supposed he should consider himself lucky, given the redhead's low opinion of him. He could have been trapped in an elevator with her instead of the huge mutt.

He sighed. This wasn't a good start to his sojourn on Central Park West.

Deciding just to mention the dog to the doorman on his way out—and perhaps work in an inquiry about the redhead—Jake shooed one of Matilda's cats off the bed. He couldn't tell the damned furballs apart. Finding them prowling about hadn't been a pleasant surprise. So much for Terrence's promise of no cats. Jake had discovered a blithe note from Matilda stuck to the refrigerator with feeding instructions and "THANK YOU" in all caps, implying he'd agreed to do the job of his own free will instead of by default. Terrence had probably told his wife that his old pal Jake was coming and she'd assumed he'd be glad to tend his cats. Terrence, being Terrence, would have neglected to tell her Jake wasn't fond of cats. Especially long-haired white cats. In the bed, no less. But now he was stuck; even he couldn't leave Apollo and Aphrodite to their own devices for a couple of weeks.

And after that wild monster in the elevator, Matilda's mannerly, well-groomed cats looked pretty good. If he could just teach them to keep off his pillow. . . .

As he headed back out into the hall, Jake kept a lookout for the galloping beast presumably still on the loose. He opted for the stairs. Not that he was a coward, but he'd only brought along so many clean shirts. Between cat hairs and dog slobber, he was going through his supply at an alarming rate.

On the stair landing, he heard the elevator slide to a halt down the hall, its doors parting smoothly, quietly.

He heard the distinct sound of dog paws on the hall's polished wood floor.

And a woman humming happily to herself.

If he moved fast, Jake thought, the dog wouldn't find him. He carefully closed the stairwell door behind him; its creak was minimal.

But suppose the mutt had pinned down another hapless victim? Or was about to? Jake hissed in disgust with all animals. Growing up, he'd had only the odd goldfish for a pet, all of whom had come to a bad end.

"Come on, Jake," came a woman's voice. "I haven't got all day. You want to chase strangers, fine. Just don't come whining to me when you're too tired to move. You've had your fun. Now hustle your butt."

This had been one hell of a strange day, and Jake had had enough. He banged open the stairwell door and marched around the corner to the elevator.

The hulking black mutt he'd met earlier loped out to greet him. Jake stood his ground. The dog's boundless energy, however, seemed depleted. He studied Jake a moment, licked his hand, then collapsed on his feet as if the two of them were old friends.

"Jake!"

What the hell was going on? A stray dog stretched out on his feet, a woman yelling at him. How did she even know he was there?

The annoyed redhead from the lobby came around the corner, hands thrust on her slender hips. She had gorgeous teal blue eyes under a tangle of curls and a tall, fit body. Her boots were caked with dried mud and her clothes reminded him of Paul Bunyan.

"Look, lady," he said, in no mood, "I don't know what your beef is with me—"

"Oh, hello," she said, cutting him off. She fastened her eyes on him and flashed a smile that would have charmed him to no end had she not just told him to hustle his butt and accused him of chasing strangers. Or had she? "You'll have to excuse my dog. He's not used to the city. You're not...um, you weren't by any chance the man in the elevator a few minutes ago?"

Jake smiled, not at all pleasantly.

"Jake really is friendly," she said.

"Jake?"

"My dog."

He stared at the homely beast. Really. He was insulted. "Where'd you get a name like that?"

"I don't know. He just looks like a Jake to me."

She wasn't helping her case any. Jake, however, was noticing she had a very attractive figure beneath her pilled, stretched sweater and near-threadbare jeans. He wished he hadn't noticed. He was certain this woman and her dog had no business in Terrence and Matilda's building on Central Park West. The doorman was probably hunting them down now. No point in his getting involved.

She nudged the beast gently with her muddy boot, her affection for the dog obvious despite her curmudgeonly way with him.

It was one ugly dog.

"Sorry if he caused you any trouble," she said as if she meant it.

"I survived."

"Do you live on this floor?"

"I'm visiting a friend," he said vaguely.

"I see. Me, too. My name's Patience, by the way," she added, as if she wasn't quite sure whether or not she should introduce herself.

Somehow he had a feeling the woman and the name didn't go together.

Jake pinned his eyes on her. She and her dog had given him a rough time and he wasn't going to let her off scot-free. "Nice to meet you, Patience," he said. "My name's Jake."

Any other self-respecting woman would have been mortified. Would have bit her lip and maybe blushed and at least said she'd had no idea that he and her ugly dog had the same name.

But redheaded Patience threw back her mass of curls and laughed a laugh that left him nearly as breathless as his ride in the elevator with her dog. It was a delicious laugh, free and uninhibited, and Jake, caught by surprise, got the hell out of there.

Yet he suspected that this wouldn't be his last encounter with Miss Patience with the muddy boots and ugly dog.

3

PATIENCE SPENT THE REST of the afternoon and early part of the evening settling into her new, mercifully temporary, quarters. Everything was very fancy. There were three beautifully decorated bedrooms, each with a private bath. There was a media room twice—maybe three times—as big as her cabin. It had a huge television screen, a state-of-the-art—or so she assumed—sound system, a CD player and various other electronic gadgets she made no attempt to identify. The library looked as if it had been imported from an English country manor. The kitchen was one heck of a lot more than two people needed: it had yards and yards of glass-fronted cabinets, blue-tiled counters, a restaurant-style stove, three sinks, two dishwashers and two English porcelain cat dishes. Jake's pocked and dented aluminum dog dish looked distinctly out of place next to Apollo and Aphrodite's dining area. The living room had a spectacular view of Central Park and the New York skyline, a couple of potted trees, original paintings Patience swore were hung upside down and more places to sit than she knew people to sit in them. The decor throughout was remarkably neutral in color, expensive, of the best quality and very, very tasteful. Things were, she had to admit, reasonably functional and comfortable. By comparison, her black-and-white television and Uncle Isaiah's old horsehair mattress looked pretty shabby.

She wondered what had happened to the Tilly Madrid who used to sleep under the Adirondack stars and tell ghost stories around the campfire.

Patience ventured out twice. First, to buy a leash for Jake. A sturdy leash. One that would keep him firmly at her side instead of leaping into elevators with good-looking men who also happened to be named Jake. Had her Jake sensed a human soul mate? Unlikely. The other Jake hadn't looked as if he appreciated dogs. Certainly he hadn't seemed to appreciate the humor in the situation. It wasn't as if her Jake had done any damage—the man had looked impossibly fit and healthy to her, especially for a New Yorker.

The second time she ventured out was to walk Jake about the neighborhood. She discovered people gave them wide berth. She also discovered she felt more damned alone walking the streets of New York, with literally millions of people all around her, than trekking around her isolated lake up in the mountains.

The doorman acted as if nothing had happened that morning.

By nightfall, she was glad to rummage in the Terwilliger library. Not a good potboiler to be found. She settled for a leather-bound, acid-free edition of *The Three Musketeers* and looked around for a spot to curl up and read. Jake, too, was on his feet, pacing, clearly not at home. There wasn't a single ratty afghan or moldy dog bone in the place. Tilly Madrid didn't stand for that sort of thing anymore now that she'd married a Terwilliger. Patience had no intention of suffering a similar fate.

"You wouldn't sacrifice a moldy dog bone for love and romance?" she could hear Tilly arguing.

But moldy dog bones were only a symbol. It was herself Patience wasn't willing to sacrifice.

Was that what Tilly had done? Had she turned into someone else just to please Terrence Terwilliger? Was that why she'd gone to Arizona alone?

You're not responsible for Tilly's happiness, Patience told herself, and, book in hand, headed to the larger of the two guest rooms. She flipped the switch just inside the door. A beautiful porcelain lamp on the Louis Quinze bedside table came on.

And she immediately spotted the wrinkled magenta men's shirt lying on the queen-size bed.

"Oh, Tilly."

She picked the shirt up with one finger and examined it. All cotton, black buttons. Pricey, but of a size and color Terrence would never wear. So were the running shoes poking out from under the bed.

Patience quickly checked the rest of the room.

A leather weekend bag—battered, beaten, ancient, and devoid of the Terwilligers' monogrammed *T*—was jammed into the closet and stuffed with clothes that couldn't possibly belong to her rich, conservative brother-in-law.

"Ah, gee, Tilly, why did you make me have to see this?"

In the adjoining bathroom, a pair of electric-blue gym shorts, a torn white T-shirt and an athletic supporter, not new, dangled from the doorknob.

"I'd take a moldy dog bone over men's exercise clothes any day," Patience muttered.

Especially *used* men's exercise clothes.

A shaving kit was unzipped on the sink. She had a peek. Razor, shaving brush, shaving cup with just a scrap of soap left in it. Toothbrush. No-wax dental floss. Generic mouthwash. After-shave. She uncorked the top and took a sniff: definitely not a Terrence Terwilliger scent. There were other more personal items she chose not to examine more closely.

"Tilly, Tilly."

None of the non-Terrence stuff was well hidden, but maybe that wasn't necessary. Maybe Terrence had already moved out. Maybe Tilly hadn't told her younger sister the truth and her marriage was pretty much over.

Tilly was having an affair.

Patience sank onto the edge of the bed. She warned herself not to jump to conclusions. But if Tilly had gone off the deep end after only a year of marriage and was seeing a man who wore magenta shirts, didn't Patience have an obligation to do something?

Like what? What did *she* know about men?

"Stop!"

Jake fled the room, but Patience was yelling at herself. Tilly was thirty-four years old and had a right to her own life. She could make her own decisions. Her own mistakes. Patience wasn't responsible for her.

Snatching up the offending magenta shirt, she marched over to the closet and stuffed the thing back into the weekender bag.

Would a lover stay in the guest room?

Tilly's would. She was scrupulous that way. Even if she and Terrence were on the skids—even if their marriage was already kaput—Tilly would refuse to entertain a lover in the same room she and her husband had shared.

Suddenly Apollo and Aphrodite appeared on the bed and began pawing the pillows, as cats, fancy Persians or not, would. They did have a peculiar charm. And they were so soft. Not like Jake. Patience could also count on them not to humiliate her the way her damned dog had.

She had to bite her lip to stop herself from laughing just thinking about it, even with the heavier issue weighing on her mind.

A vision of the other Jake—the human one—worked its way to the forefront of her mind, as it had far too often over the course of the day. She didn't want to think about how her Jake seemed to have taken a liking to him—and how she herself kept thinking about him and his dark eyes.

She climbed into bed, determined to enjoy her elegant surroundings and solitude.

But she could see the electric-blue gym shorts hanging on the bathroom doorknob.

Men.

Unable to stand it another second, Patience jumped out of bed, marched into the bathroom, grabbed the toilet brush, and, using the handle, removed the offending articles of clothing from the doorknob. Holding them at arm's length, she deposited them unceremoniously on the closet floor. Then she took a shower, dropping the shampoo bottle on her toe and spilling it. The cap hadn't been screwed on tight. When Tilly got back from Arizona, she told herself, the two of them would go out to dinner and talk. *Really* talk. Not about Patience's love life—or lack thereof—for a change, but about what was going on in Tilly's apparently overactive love life.

How could her sister take up with a man who left the cap loose on the shampoo?

To add to her annoyance, when she climbed out of the shower Patience realized she'd forgotten her nightgown. She'd already turned the heat in the Terwilligers' apartment down to sixty degrees. She hated hot buildings, and there was no point in wasting energy. Why else was flannel invented if not for cool nights? Streaking naked into the guest room, she grabbed a berry-colored T-shirt from the interloper's bag. Definitely not a Terrence Terwilliger color. It wasn't one of her colors, either. It clashed with her hair, but with only two Persian cats and a dog to notice, she put it on and climbed into bed with *The Three Musketeers*.

Jake—all hundred pounds of him—jumped into bed with her and the two cats, who'd already made themselves at home. They didn't seem too sure about her dog, but weren't willing to give up a warm bed.

Ordinarily Patience would have shoved Jake back onto the floor where he belonged, but New York was a strange place for him, and for her, too. She switched on the bedside radio and tried not to feel as if she'd just landed on the moon. Outside, New York was aglow. It wasn't like the Adirondacks at all.

An hour or so later, D'Artagnan was taking France by storm when Jake suddenly leaped off the bed and bounded out of the room. Patience paid no attention. Jake was forever chasing mythical rabbits.

"My God," a man yelled from somewhere in the cavernous apartment, "where did *you* come from?"

Patience bolted upright in bed, her heart racing. She threw down her book. She could hear Jake growling. A burglar? Surely not. Jake would have responded sooner. She'd locked the doors . . .

But I didn't do the chain lock!

What were doormen for if not to intercept burglars?

Maybe it was Tilly's lover.

It was almost midnight. Without making a sound, hoping Jake wouldn't give her away, Patience reached for the bedside phone. She'd call the doorman.

"Nice dog. You remember me, don't you?"

Her hand stopped midair. Remember him?

"Patience?"

"Ah, gee," she muttered, "this can't be."

"Patience, are you in here somewhere? Call off this monster, will you?"

But it was. The man from the elevator. The other Jake. He must be friends with Tilly and Terrence and have his own key. Why the devil hadn't her sister warned her?

She didn't call Jake off right away. This was no time to be jumping to conclusions. He might *not* be a friend of Tilly and Terrence. "What do you want?" she called out.

"What do you mean?" He sounded annoyed. "I want to stay in one piece!"

Obviously he wasn't a dog person. A dog person would have known Jake was harmless. Patience remained wary. "How do I know you're not a criminal?"

Before she could answer, Jake galloped back into the guest room all excited and leaped onto the bed. She thought the slats would give out. He stayed on all fours, breathing in her face. He wasn't one to growl for long. He had no attention span.

The other Jake stood in the doorway. He had his arms crossed over his chest, and his dark eyes focused directly—unswervingly—on Patience.

"You," he said darkly, "must be Matilda's younger sister."

It wasn't easy to be dignified in bed with a dog and two cats and a berry-colored T-shirt that didn't go with her hair, but Patience did her best. She tried not to pay any attention to the way her visitor slouched against the doorjamb, the way his square jaw was set hard as he studied her.

"That's right," she said. She shoved Jake down. "We met earlier today, remember?"

"Oh, I remember." His tone suggested it wasn't anything he was soon likely to forget. "Nobody told me you were coming."

"Should anyone have?"

His dark eyes narrowed even more. He wasn't a happy individual; clearly she and her dog weren't a pleasant surprise. Patience took stock of his blue cotton shirt and canvas pants. *This* was a man who'd wear a magenta shirt and hang his exercise clothes on a doorknob.

He said tightly, "I would have thought so."

She tried to be diplomatic. "I don't tell my friends every little thing, either. Now if you don't mind—"

"Obviously, you weren't told anything about me."

She stared, her stomach twisting. "What?"

"If *you* don't mind, I'd like you and those animals out of my bed."

"*Your* bed?" *Oh, Tilly.*

"My bed. The way I see it, first come, first serve. And that's *my* shirt you're wearing. I'd like you out of it, too." He added quickly, not one drop of color coming into his face, "And into something else."

The man was proprietary, to say the least. "What makes you so sure this is your shirt? I know lots of people who have raspberry T-shirts."

His eyes nailed her right to the mattress. "And I'd lay odds with that hair of yours you're not one of them."

"Well, nobody says it's yours—"

"Would you like me to go over there and *prove* it's mine?"

He would do it, too. Patience could see he was at his wits' end, thrown completely off balance by her presence. Not by her necessarily, but by the simple fact of her. As if finding a strange woman in his bed was the last straw.

She, however, wasn't a woman easily intimidated, especially when she had Jake—*her* Jake—licking his chops beside her. He was doing it just because he was tired and thirsty, but that other Jake, not being a dog person, couldn't know that. And he—the four-legged Jake—did look menacing.

Of course, when it came right down to it, so did the human Jake. He wasn't a handsome man. Not ugly by any means. Just no fair-haired Terrence Terwilliger III. He had that square, imposing jaw and those dark, menacing eyes, plus high cheekbones, thick hair, and an athletic build. She tried to picture him in a pin-striped suit and found, oddly, that she could, although it didn't soften him.

She wondered if his temperament and looks were as incongruous as her dog's were.

"And don't think," he said, "that slobbering mutt of yours would stop me."

It was just the sort of know-it-all, authoritative, macho attitude that didn't work with Patience. She stretched out her long legs under the covers and, deliberately and obviously, leaned back against the pillows and yawned. She'd lay odds she and the man in the doorway were the same height. Whoever he was, he wasn't as refined as Tilly's husband, wouldn't limit his library to books by dead authors. He'd have a good international thriller or two on his bookshelves.

Her sister had never fallen for anyone remotely so... Patience couldn't quite put her finger on *what* this Jake character was.

It was almost midnight, and there were animals and a strange woman in what he claimed was his bed. Well, what did he think *she* was feeling? Did he think she enjoyed having a strange man pop in on her and start making demands?

"I've heard all about you," he said ominously. "I'm not backing down."

So her reputation had preceded her. If Tilly had been telling tales, it was no wonder the man hadn't backed off. Tilly liked to paint her younger sister as something of a female Paul Bunyan of the Adirondacks to her New York friends. If Jake believed even half of what Tilly was likely to have told him—and probably not even half was true—he wouldn't worry a whole lot about scaring her half to death, which, Patience suddenly realized, he hadn't.

"Wait in the kitchen," she told him. She wasn't about to let him get away with doing all the ordering. "I'll be out in a minute."

"Make it a fast minute."

A man who liked to have the last word. Patience let him have it. She watched him about-face and head out into the hall. She could have sicced her dog on him, she supposed, but the man was in no mood and her poor mutt had had enough excitement and endured enough insults for one day.

And more to the point, Patience herself wasn't in the mood. Her zest for combat had evaporated.

Tilly's Jake, she thought, was, in addition to everything else, one intensely sexy man. The kind who'd have his way with a wealthy married woman, take her for what he could get and dump her. Tilly just wasn't savvy. She trusted people too easily. If Patience was going to find out what was going on between her sister and this character, *she* had to be savvy.

She also had to be dressed in something besides the man's shirt.

"Oh, Til, what have you gotten yourself into?"

Patience scrambled for her jeans, a sweatshirt and socks. Then she headed to the kitchen with the four-legged Jake at her side, not standing guard, she knew, but just looking for scraps. The other Jake, however, didn't have to know that.

JAKE FOUND A BOTTLE of Saranac beer in the Terwilligers' refrigerator, opened it, took as big a gulp as he could without spilling it all over his face and pulled out a chair at the antique country pine table.

He had never in his life experienced anything like today. Hoodwinked into taking care of Matilda's cats. Trapped in an elevator with a monstrous, ugly, smelly, slobbering hound. Screamed at by a crazy redhead. Only she'd turned out not to be screaming at him, but at her dog, who went by the same name.

Once off Central Park West, he'd had a relatively ordinary Saturday, running errands, checking on his apartment, stopping by his office to do a few things, having dinner and catching a movie with a friend going through a divorce. He'd looked forward to shutting the cats out of his bedroom and having a relaxing hour or two before hitting the sheets.

Now this.

Patience Madrid in his T-shirt and in his bed.

Patience Madrid, a dog and two cats in his bed.

Why the hell hadn't Terrence warned him? It was possible, he supposed, that he and Matilda had gotten their wires crossed and inadvertently neglected to tell Jake he'd have to share their apartment with a nutty redhead and her dog. But why did he feel as if he'd been had?

He drank more of his beer. The redhead with the unruly dog didn't resemble the image he'd had of Matilda Terwilliger's eccentric younger sister. If she did, he might have figured out who she was sooner.

But Patience Madrid—Jake didn't think he'd ever heard her name before—was supposed to, well, not have such startlingly teal eyes, such dark lashes, such a mane of untamed strawberry hair. Unlike her older sister, Patience wasn't a delicate woman. Feminine, yes. He'd have had to be blind not to have noticed the soft curves under the T-shirt. But she wasn't fragile. She couldn't be, he supposed, and live the strange life Matilda had described her as leading.

"She's a freelance writer specializing in the environment," he recalled Matilda having told him. "I think she gets along better with animals than she does with people. Sometimes I'm afraid she's going to become a hermit like Uncle Isaiah. Did you know he never ventured further south than the Catskills in his whole life?"

An odd family. From what Jake could gather, Terrence had snapped up the only normal one of the bunch. Uncle Isaiah was dead, but the parents, last Jake had heard, were off on some archaeological dig on the shores of the Black Sea, and there were more uncles, aunts and cousins—none normal.

The dog trotted into the Terwilligers' airy, attractive kitchen, interrupting Jake's thoughts. He refused to let the beast unnerve him. He'd come face to face with a large bear once in the Canadian Rockies and had hardly flinched. Patience Madrid's ratty-looking dog wasn't going to be his undoing. Besides, if the creature hadn't eaten him by now, surely he wouldn't bother in the near future.

"Better watch out," his unexpected roommate said, coming into the kitchen. "Jake likes beer."

"He would," Jake said.

"But he's not particular. I usually keep a six-pack of the cheap stuff around just for him. I guess that's one area where he's different from you."

Jake would suggest there were considerably more areas of difference besides their beer-drinking habits. He had no idea, however, whether or not to believe anything Patience Madrid said. He watched her move to the refrigerator with surprising grace for a woman rumored to chop her own wood and shoot her own game. She got out a beer—for herself or for the dog, Jake wasn't sure. She opened it without struggle and poured a little into a pottery mixing bowl on the floor next to the cats' dishes and a battered aluminum dish filled with dry dog food. Jake thought he remembered Matilda serving pasta in that same bowl—it was made in Portugal, as he recalled—some weeks ago at one of her small dinner parties.

"I didn't bring a water dish," Patience said by way of explanation, then sat across from him at the table and started on the rest of her beer. "I never can drink a whole one."

"So you drink the cheap stuff as well?"

She smiled. Her teeth were white and even and she appeared to have all of them; apparently she believed in modern medicine enough to visit a dentist. Matilda had claimed her sister was an expert in herbal potions. Jake was beginning to suspect she'd exaggerated Patience's life-style to spice up dinner-party conversation. Then again, maybe she hadn't.

"I don't have discerning taste buds when it comes to beer," Patience Madrid said.

From what he'd gathered from scraps of conversation with Matilda and Terrence, she didn't have discerning tastes in anything but men. "God forbid you should ever tangle with Matilda's sister," Terrence had said. "Let me tell you, I don't lie awake nights worrying about her living up in the mountains alone. Anyone pestering her—man or beast—is likely to end up hanging on a meat hook in her woodshed."

Apparently her romantic life didn't measure up to bringing home a wounded baby moose or writing articles on the migratory patterns of northeastern songbirds. But she seemed happy enough to Jake. He was something of a loner himself and not inclined to think a person couldn't live a fulfilling life unless married with two-point-three children, or whatever the current average was.

"I'm afraid you have me at something of a disadvantage." Her sudden formality caught him off guard. She looked incredibly *in*formal in her bulky pumpkin sweatshirt and jeans. His T-shirt had been considerably sexier on her. But her teal eyes, he noticed, were soft, curious and—he wasn't a hundred percent sure of this—challenging, even a little unfriendly. What the hell had *he* done? She went on in that same formal tone, "All I know about you is that your name is Jake."

"I see." He was just as glad Matilda hadn't carried north the same sort of stories about him as she'd told about her sister. "I'm Jake Farr, a friend of your sister's."

"Oh, I gathered that much."

Her tone sharpened. Jake finished off the last of his beer, studying her. Definitely a complex woman. There was an air of intelligence and sophistication about her that he just wouldn't have expected from someone who lived the life she lived. "Is something wrong?" he asked.

She bristled. "Mr. Farr, I'll tell you straight out that I don't like to play games."

"Look," he said, attempting to sound reasonable. He pushed back his chair in case she decided to throw something at him, which, given her tone, was entirely possible. "This has been a confusing day for both of us. If you want to spell out just where it is you're coming from, go right ahead. No need for either of us to play games."

Patience sat forward in her chair, but avoided his eyes. "Tilly didn't tell you I was coming?"

Jake tried to hold back a smile. Tilly? He couldn't imagine refined, delicate Matilda Terwilliger answering to a name like Tilly. Of course, he couldn't imagine anyone thinking a hairy mutt like the one who'd lapped up beer and collapsed at his feet looked like a Jake.

He shook his head. "I had no idea."

"She should have told you—or at least told me about you two. Not that I hadn't guessed something was going on."

"I beg your pardon?"

Her cheeks were peachy-red, an accomplishment for a woman who didn't appear to embarrass easily, if at all. "I take it Terrence doesn't know?"

"About me? Of course Terrence knows about me. He and I have been friends since nursery school. He's the one who invited me to stay here while he was away."

"Oh." Patience smiled feebly. "This has been a confusing day."

It wasn't getting any less confusing, either. "Who'd you think I was?"

She waved a hand. "Never mind. Why did Terrence invite you to stay here?"

"My apartment's being renovated and a trip I was supposed to go on fell through." Didn't materialize was more like it, but it was a fine point, too fine a point to try to make at one o'clock in the morning with a giant dog asleep on his feet and a teal-eyed redhead staring him down. "He didn't mention you'd be staying here as well, and I didn't have a chance to see Matilda before they left."

Patience Madrid exhaled, suddenly looking tired. "This is nuts."

"I gather you're supposed to be taking the cats up to the country while Matilda's gone?"

"No, Tilly would never allow her precious kitties to spend ten minutes up north with me. No, she—" But Patience stopped herself midsentence and went tight-lipped on him, apparently unwilling to talk further about her sister. As if Matilda had anything to hide! "The way I see it, all we have here is a failure to communicate. It's no big deal. Doesn't matter what you thought or what I thought. Me and Jake—" this time when she paused she grinned "—have come to the big city to cat-sit. That's all."

"Well," Jake said, rising, "you're welcome to Mr. Apollo and Ms. Aphrodite. I'm not a cat person."

"No kidding." Her tone was richly sarcastic. "What're you going to do?"

He set his empty beer bottle on the counter. Patience, he noticed, hadn't yet finished hers. Maybe she was waiting for him to leave so she could give the rest to the dog. He said, "There's not much I can do tonight. It's late and I'm tired."

She fastened her wide, black-lashed, curiously mesmerizing eyes on him. "I suppose you want your bed back?"

Oh, lady, he thought. Do you know how attractive you are or do you just not care? "I imagine it's full of dog and cat hair by now."

"Are you allergic or something?"

It amazed him that pet-lovers couldn't fathom how some people might not want to inhale dander and dried saliva and animal hair all night. "You can keep your bed," he said diplomatically. "The other guest room's not made up. I'll just sleep in the den."

She didn't argue with him, and as Jake left the kitchen, wondering why the hell he didn't just cut his losses, go home, uncover his own damned bed and sleep there, he glanced back and saw Patience Madrid pour the rest of her beer in the Terwilligers' handcrafted Portuguese pottery bowl for her ugly dog. Somehow he thought that Terrence didn't have the faintest idea that his sister-in-law had taken up residence in the apartment. So what were Matilda Madrid Terwilliger and her teal-eyed little sister up to?

Jake snuck back into the guest room for his bag and kit, noting with some annoyance that Patience had taken over the bathroom with her glycerin soap, wood-handled toothbrush and non-animal-tested moisturizer. Hadn't the woman seen his stuff and figured there might be another guest staying in her sister's apartment?

He found his sweats in a heap in the closet and gritted his teeth.

And then it hit him.

"She should have told you—or at least told me about you two. Not that I hadn't guessed something was going on."

Good God! The lunatic had thought that he and Matilda . . . that he and her sister . . . that he and Terrence's wife . . .

He took his things and stomped back to the den, then kicked off his shoes and flopped back on the long leather couch. He and Matilda as . . .

It was crazy!

And then he began to laugh, hard.

"It's not that damned funny," Patience Madrid yelled from down the hall. "Anybody could've made such a mistake."

Now, how had she known what he was laughing about? Jake sat up straight. "Are you kidding? Terrence and I have been friends for years. I'd never have an affair with his wife."

"How was I supposed to know that? Terrence is such a stuffed shirt and you're . . . not."

"Couldn't you look at me and know I'm not even remotely your sister's type?"

Patience Madrid didn't answer.

And Jake grinned. This time he really couldn't help himself. He was grinning because, for what was the first and probably the last time, he knew exactly what the crazy, sexy redhead was thinking: he might not be her sister's type, but he sure was *her* type. And that would bother a woman like Patience Madrid a whole lot more than she'd like it to.

As he settled back into the buttery-soft leather cushions, her maddening dog pranced in, collapsing in a heap on the floor just below Jake's nose. He smelled like he'd been chasing New Yorkers all day.

"Go on, you."

The pea-brained beast ignored him.

Jake groaned and rolled onto his back so his nose wouldn't be within smelling range of his unwanted companion.

"Terrence, my friend," he said half-aloud, "do you know what your wife has done to me?"

Or had Terrence been a party to the conspiracy as well? *Was* it a conspiracy? Patience Madrid, her ugly dog Jake, two Persian cats. With friends like the Terwilligers, who the hell needed enemies?

The dog fell asleep first.

Jake had peeled down to his underwear and wrapped himself tightly in a cashmere throw, but he couldn't get warm. It was a damned refrigerator in the apartment. Finally, he checked the thermostat. Sixty degrees! No wonder he was freezing! He knew Terrence was a tightwad, but this was inhuman. He turned the temperature up to sixty-eight and went back to bed, and as he drifted off, he found himself picturing Patience Madrid snuggled under the covers of the bed where he should be sleeping.

It was a disturbing picture, but nothing like a nightmare. He relaxed, his confusion lessening. Perhaps it hadn't been such a rotten, miserable day after all, but only a very interesting one. Then he found himself wondering something that would undoubtedly make his friend Terrence happy since it showed he wasn't bored.

He was wondering, simply, what tomorrow would bring.

4

PATIENCE MADE AN ENORMOUS breakfast of oatmeal pancakes, fresh fruit and coffee. Lots of coffee. She'd had a bad night. The prospect of facing Jake Farr after her erroneous deduction that he and Tilly had something going had kept her tossing and turning. So had her own distrust of her sister. Just because Tilly and Terrence were having marital problems didn't mean she was having an affair! Patience had no idea what had gotten into her. Probably just being in New York.

Jake, the traitor, wandered into the kitchen and dropped onto her feet as she spooned pancakes onto the griddle. He'd never returned to her bedroom, but presumably had spent the night with his human counterpart. She'd only had Tilly's cats for company.

"Yeah," she said, "now that you're hungry you show up."

But she never could hold a grudge and tossed him a pancake. He downed it in a single gulp and stayed close to her in case she had another attack of generosity.

"Is your pal up?" she asked.

She looked at Jake as if he just might answer. It was a bad habit. In her view there was nothing wrong with talking to animals. She didn't want to ignore the dog, risk his getting lonely. Tilly insisted her sister needed human company. "What you need," she'd told Patience at least a thousand times, "is someone who'll talk *back*."

She flipped on the radio to catch the morning news. Who said she didn't have human contact?

In a couple of hours, when Tilly, in Mountain Standard Time, was more likely to be up, she'd receive a call from her younger sister about who else was sharing her Central Park West apartment.

Patience flipped the bubbling pancakes. A good breakfast would help put her in a proper frame of mind.

Jake Farr stumbled into the kitchen and nearly took her breath away with his unbridled masculinity, the intimacy his presence could so easily have implied. He had on jeans with no belt and his blue cotton shirt, unbuttoned, untucked, open at the cuffs, revealing his flat stomach and the dark hairs on his chest.

"Good morning," she said, aware of the catch in her voice. She just wasn't used to having men around at breakfast.

He looked stiff, half-asleep, grumpy. "What the hell time is it?"

Patience glanced at the clock radio. "Seven-thirty."

"It's Sunday morning."

"Yes, it is."

"Don't you sleep late on Sundays?"

"Well, yes. I see you do, too."

"Seven-thirty," he said, "is *not* my idea of late." He squinted at her, his dark eyes obviously not ready to be fully open. "What the hell time do you usually get up?"

She shrugged, refusing to be embarrassed by the routines that had stood her in good stead for thirty-two years. "Five-thirty or sunup, whichever comes first. I get my best writing done in the morning. I woke you up?"

"You woke your dog up, who woke me up by licking my face."

"Licking your face?" She grinned at her dog. "And I thought you were a one-person dog, Jake. You know, he doesn't usually take to strangers."

Clearly not a morning person, Jake Farr grunted, eyeing the coffeepot. Patience told him to help himself, which he did. She wondered if he'd reacted to her as she had to him. Doubtful. She just didn't have the ability to look terrific in a borrowed men's flannel nightshirt—Terrence would probably never forgive her—and wool socks, hair uncombed, face just splashed with cold water. Some women probably could, but not her. She'd pulled her hair back with a rubber band just to keep it off her face while she cooked. Tilly would be horrified. Last Christmas she'd sent Patience a ton of pricey cosmetics, a make-over book and a dozen different kinds of barrettes, ribbons and headbands. Patience had been more amused than insulted. Did Tilly think she didn't know how to dress up? Just because she didn't do it often didn't mean she didn't know how. She wasn't a total hermit. She'd just had a working winter was all.

Nevertheless, she was just as glad she was in no condition to appeal to Jake Farr. That would only complicate matters.

"Would you like some pancakes?" she asked politely.

Standing over her, he studied the griddle dubiously.

"I've got pure maple syrup, too. Made it myself. I stuck a pint in my suitcase when I headed south."

He seemed to be picturing her hauling buckets of sap, which is exactly what she'd been doing last weekend. She doubted it required a great leap of imagination.

"Sounds good."

Without another word, he set the table, finding his way around the Terwilliger kitchen with little difficulty. He even put out cloth napkins and poured the syrup into a small Bennington pottery pitcher. Patience was impressed.

"No nuts and seeds in the pancakes?" he asked.

"Nope."

They were, in fact, light and sweet, tasting faintly of oatmeal.

After two pancakes, Jake said, "There's no need for me to intrude on your stay in New York. I'll head out this morning and leave you to your dog and your sister's cats."

Patience fought back a totally ridiculous sense of disappointment. What, honestly, had she expected? Or wanted? "Where will you stay?"

"New York has an abundance of hotels."

"You're welcome here, you know." She might as well be polite, since there was obviously no way he'd stay. And wasn't that just as well? He really was a distraction she didn't need right now. "I don't want Terrence accusing me of driving you out. He . . . Did he not know I'd be here?"

Jake gave her a dry look. "I'd say most certainly not."

"You're sure he'd have told you?"

"If he'd expected us to remain friends, I would hope so."

Patience decided it was just as well she wasn't the touchy type or she might have been insulted. It wasn't as if Jake Farr had found himself camped out with a nest of poisonous snakes. Then again, maybe he'd have preferred snakes to her, her dog and Tilly's cats.

"What about Tilly?" she asked.

"Matilda didn't mention you, either, but I didn't see her before she left." He buttered a third pancake. "I'm assuming this ordeal is simply the result of the right hand not knowing what the left hand's up to."

Ordeal? Patience didn't pursue his assessment of their situation, but in the silence that followed she became aware of Jake Farr's deep brown eyes boring into her. It was decidedly unsettling. Made her wish she'd put a bra on before heading into the kitchen.

She called him on it. "Something on your mind, Mr. Farr?"

He averted his gaze and swallowed another forkful of pancakes. Jake—the dog—moved in closer, looking hopeful.

She'd given up on getting an answer when Jake Farr asked abruptly, "Why did you jump to the conclusion that Matilda and I . . . that we . . ."

"Because I'm an idiot," Patience said, not one to air the family laundry in front of strangers.

"You must have been predisposed to think she was—"

Patience jumped up. "I'd forget what I said if I were you. I was flustered and just grasped at straws."

"Well," he said, setting down his fork, "I'm sure Terrence and Matilda are having a wonderful time in Florida."

So Jake Farr didn't know they'd gone on separate vacations. Probably Tilly had confided in Patience just because of her cats, and now she'd blurted out her fears to Terrence's best friend. Or a friend, anyway. How could a "best" friend not know Terrence was having marital troubles?

"I'm sure they are," she said.

Her unexpected roommate sighed and stood up. "I'll do the dishes," he said. "Then I'll be on my way. What are your plans for the day?"

Calling Tilly and doing her best to wring her neck long distance. To him, however, she said, "I don't know. Read the paper and work on an article I brought along. Look, as I said, you don't have to leave. It's not as if there's not enough room for the two of us."

"The five of us," Jake Farr corrected.

Apollo and Aphrodite, Patience had already observed, only entered the kitchen at mealtime. They were pampered and regal—not like real cats at all. They'd probably call 911 if they ever saw a mouse.

"*I* could leave," she offered. "I could bring the cats up north with me. Tilly would never know. Then you could have the place to yourself."

"That would never do."

"I just don't want you to feel as if I've run you out."

Jake Farr looked at her. "Patience, do you want me to stay?"

"Well, if you have no other alternative . . ."

"Oh, I always have alternatives."

And he smiled a secret, sexy smile that made her wonder just what the man was thinking. Or could he read her thoughts? Did he know that she was reacting to him in a way that could only be explained by the long, cold winter?

He didn't say anything, just rolled up his sleeves and started on the breakfast dishes.

"YOU RAN HIM OFF ALREADY? Honestly, Patience, you're impossible."

Tilly sounded disgusted. Jake Farr had been gone an hour—he'd packed up his shaving kit, sweat clothes, magenta shirt, everything. Patience had been about to put a call through to Arizona when the telephone rang: her sister checking up on her cats.

"I didn't run him off," she said. "He left of his own accord. How come you didn't warn me about him?"

"Because I didn't know he'd be there. It was Terrence's idea—I hadn't told him you'd be cat-sitting."

"Does he know now?"

"Not yet, unless Jake's told him."

"I wouldn't think he'd bother. He seemed to be glad to be out of here."

"What did you do to him?"

"What do you mean, what did I do to him? Tilly, just because my love life isn't the stuff of romance novels doesn't mean I'm a jerk. He thought I stole his bed and—"

"His bed? Patience, what went on there?"

"Don't get any ideas. And if he tells you I stole his shirt, don't believe him. He left with everything he came in with, I assure you."

"I see," Tilly said, clearly not seeing at all.

Patience wished she hadn't even tried to explain. "Jake Farr thinks you and Terrence are in Florida together."

"Terrence doesn't like to discuss his personal problems with anyone, even his best friend." She quickly changed the subject. "How're Apollo and Aphrodite?"

"Just dandy."

"What did you end up doing with Jake?"

"Jake?"

"Your dog, Patience."

"Oh, he—"

But Patience had never been an adept liar, and Tilly was onto her immediately. "You brought him with you, didn't you? Oh, Patience, how could you? No wonder Jake left. Nobody but you can stand that dog."

"He's a great dog."

"Outside, maybe. But not inside. Not in New York, Patience. He didn't— He hasn't done anything, has he?"

Patience had already decided not to tell her sister about Jake's entrance yesterday morning. "On the whole he's been remarkably well behaved."

"That could mean anything. Jake hates dogs—"

"He does not. He's fine with other dogs."

"I don't mean your Jake. Oh, hell." Now she was sounding like the old Tilly. "What a mess."

"It's not a mess. Me and Jake and the cats are all fine. Jake Farr's gone home, or to a hotel, anyway. He's out of here. So you just relax and enjoy your vacation and don't worry about a thing."

"You're sure?"

She sounded almost desperate. Patience's tone softened. "Of course."

"Well, okay."

"Do you have the number where you're staying? I was going to call you earlier, but I realized I didn't have your number. I don't even know the name of your hotel."

"The Hidden Camel Resort in Scottsdale. I'm at the pool, so I don't have the number handy. You can get it from information or I'll give it to you next time I call. Have fun and do *not* give that confounded dog of yours any of our Saranac beer. It's Terrence's favorite."

She and Jake had just split one while she did the *New York Times* crossword puzzle. "Anything else?"

"Enjoy New York."

And for no reason that she could think of, Patience thought of Jake Farr as she hung up the phone. What on earth did he have to do with her enjoying New York? Likely enough, she'd never see the man again.

Which, it had seemed to her, was just fine with him.

She grabbed the new leash. "Come on, Jake. Let's go for a walk."

But he didn't answer back and, much as she liked the hairy mutt, he just didn't have Jake Farr's dark eyes, his square jaw, his muscular thighs.

"Egad," she muttered, "are you sure you're going to be able to stand two weeks of New York if this is what it does to you?"

She snapped the leash onto Jake's collar, and they headed out together.

"JAKE, SOMETHING STRANGE is going on."

It was late Sunday evening and Jake was on the phone in the middle of the unholy mess that had become his apartment. He didn't dare sit anywhere. All day, in fact, he'd felt out of sorts, as if he didn't know where the hell he was welcome, even where he belonged.

"You're not kidding," he told Terrence. "You didn't warn me about Apollo, Aphrodite, Jake and Patience Madrid."

"Jake? Oh, God, she has that damned dog of hers in our apartment! Matilda didn't tell me—" He broke off with a slight growl, regaining his impressive self-control. "I apologize for the confusion. Matilda and I really messed up on this one. Patience came down from the mountains to watch the cats—I didn't realize until we'd already left."

"That's okay. What's done is done. I made good my escape this morning."

And it *had* been an escape, he'd decided. Not the deliberate choice he'd pretended it was. He'd fled from Patience Madrid and her wild red hair, teal eyes and hearty, free laugh. All day he'd been fighting the nagging sense that he'd been a coward. But in what way? It wasn't as if he knew the woman, owed her anything or had done anything to her.

But maybe he'd done something to himself.

"So I gather," Terrence said. "Matilda phoned Patience earlier in the day and, well, to be blunt, she asked me to ask you to look in on her sister while she's in New York. Apparently Patience has been having a tough go of it lately and seems a little depressed. I don't have the specifics, but I gather she's had some trouble with her work and shut herself up in her cabin most of the winter. Matilda hopes she can take advantage of being in the city to relax and see people, have some fun, but so far she shows no indication of wanting to leave the apartment."

Jake contemplated his friend's words, but they just didn't jive. Something was going on. "Out with it, Terrence. You're leading up to asking a favor, aren't you?"

Terrence sighed in a long-suffering way that Jake imagined was a symptom of living with a Madrid—even one as sweet as Matilda. "Matilda wants you to go back to the apartment. Just be a friend for Patience. I know it's asking a lot, Jake, but I also know staying at your apartment is virtually impossible. Look, there's nothing underhanded here. You've seen Patience. It's not like Matilda would try to fix you two up or anything."

"Then what *is* she trying to do?"

"Help her sister."

"Have *me* help her sister, you mean. Terrence, I don't know the woman, but, if you ask me, there didn't seem a damned thing wrong with Patience Madrid except her choice of names for that ugly dog of hers."

Terrence laughed. "He is homely, isn't he?"

But, in the end, Jake was persuaded. He had no idea why. But he decided he had nothing to lose by offering the woman his company. Besides, Matilda and Terrence had never asked him such a favor before.

"It's important," Terrence stressed.

"What do you think of this Patience character?" Jake asked, trying to shove aside an image of her wide, clear eyes and be more objective.

"I think," his friend said carefully, "that Matilda is probably overreacting, and if I were you I'd watch myself. Patience Madrid is probably the most stubbornly self-sufficient and totally irascible woman I've ever met."

Even with what little he knew about her, Jake was inclined to agree. But he'd have to add curiously beautiful—with her eye-catching curves and mass of red tangles—something he couldn't have expected Terrence to notice, married as he was to her older sister.

And, Jake thought, Patience Madrid was a hell of a lot more interesting than his empty, torn-apart apartment.

"At least she's not boring," Terrence said.

"*That* she's not."

"I owe you, Jake. I wouldn't ask something like this of you if Matilda didn't seem so desperate. I've never seen her so worried about her sister."

"But you don't share her concerns?"

"To be honest with you, I don't know. I just think the whole thing is strange. Patience has always seemed to me to have life by the tail. You will watch yourself with her?"

Jake laughed. "It's okay, Terrence. I'm a big boy. I can handle Patience Madrid."

Terrence Terwilliger made no further comment on the subject of his sister-in-law, but simply wished him well—and good luck.

By EARLY EVENING, Patience was back in Terrence's nightshirt and had a fire going in the library as she snuggled under a cashmere throw and pored through a few more chapters of *The Three Musketeers*. But for the occasional image of Jake Farr flashing in her mind, she'd had a good day. She'd gone out to walk Jake and pick up groceries, but had decided "doing" New York could wait for another day, if she bothered at all. She needed time to get over having had and lost her interesting, if hard to figure, roommate.

Then the doorman called up and announced a Mr. Farr was in the lobby and did she want to see him?

"What for?" she asked.

"Just a moment, Miss Madrid, and I'll inquire."

She waited a few moments.

"Mr. Farr, er, wishes to spend the night."

Not one to embarrass easily, Patience nonetheless felt her cheeks heat up. Did Jake think he was funny? Or was he deliberately trying to get to her? *I could send him on his way.* But he was Tilly and Terrence's friend. And she wouldn't mind a chance to prove to her sister that she, Patience, wasn't a total hermit and could stand a roommate for a few days. Even one who hated animals and was as darkly sexy as Jake Farr.

"Send him up," she told the doorman as coolly and smoothly as she could manage.

She decided not to wait for him in the doorway, lest he get the idea she was panting for him or something, but stayed put until he rang the doorbell. With the throw around her shoulders and her four-legged roommates trailing behind her, she walked unhurriedly into the gleaming foyer, undid the series of locks, and, making no self-conscious effort to push the strawberry tangles from her face, let Jake Farr in.

It was like opening the door to the desert wind. The effect of the man hit her full force. He'd exchanged his jeans and cotton shirt for charcoal-gray canvas pants and a madras shirt, with a slouchy black leather jacket and scuffed boots. He did not look urbane. He did not look like Terrence Terwilliger III's best friend.

Patience couldn't remember being so affected by a man. Had to be New York. Too much ozone in the air or something.

She noted the same battered suitcase he'd carried out with him that morning.

"Hi," he said. "I'm back."

No kidding. She managed a smile and hugged the throw around her. She felt like Cinderella before her fairy godmother showed up. Probably should have rubbed ashes on her face before coming to the door. At least her brother-in-law's taste in nightshirts meant heavy flannel. Most of hers were pilled and frayed, but still, at least so far as she was concerned, had plenty of wear.

"Turns out my apartment's unlivable, and there isn't a decent hotel room available in New York. Lots of indecent ones, but—"

"You don't have to explain," she said, cool, collected, a hell of a lot less naive than Cinderella. "It's not my place to turn you out. I'm Tilly's sister and you're Terrence's friend. I guess we both have a right to be here."

Didn't that sound reasonable? So why, she wondered, was her heart skipping along at an alarming rate?

Jake Farr said, "I'll try to find someplace else to stay tomorrow."

"Don't worry about it. Think you can stand Jake?"

Her incorrigible dog had already greeted their visitor in his wholehearted way—by jumping up and placing his paws on Jake's chest. At least he wasn't dirty. Patience had cleaned him up that morning for his sojourn in the big city. Firmly, but reasonably gently, Jake Farr shoved his new friend back down onto all fours and told him to sit. Patience didn't elucidate on the total unlikelihood of Jake's obeying ninety percent of his—or anyone's—commands.

He didn't so much sit as collapse.

"Good dog," Jake Farr said, half-heartedly. He looked at Patience and added without enthusiasm, "I can stand him."

"And Apollo and Aphrodite?"

He nodded curtly, and took his suitcase down to the second guest room, Jake trotting happily behind him.

Patience hadn't, of course, made up the bed. And wouldn't. Jake Farr looked perfectly capable of putting sheets on a bed. Before leaving on her private vacation, Tilly had offered to have her housekeeper come by, but Patience had turned her down, preferring to clean up after herself. Also, she'd had her doubts from the start whether she'd be able to leave Jake and hadn't wanted to have any spies reporting back to her sister. Besides, a housekeeper would probably not react well to a four-legged surprise like Jake.

Leaving her roommate to his own devices, she returned to the library with *The Three Musketeers*. Apollo had perched himself on the back of the leather couch. Aphrodite jumped onto Patience's lap and made herself at home. Jake, the traitor, had abandoned her.

It wasn't long—just a few pages of mayhem in seventeenth-century France—before she became aware of a human presence in the library. Looking up from her book, she saw Jake Farr leaning against the doorjamb. Her dog squeezed past him and collapsed on the rug in front of the couch, exhaling as if he'd run around the lake at home instead of just having greeted a guest. One day in New York and already he was getting soft.

New York, however, hadn't seemed to make Jake Farr soft. His sweater loosely outlined the width of his chest and the bulk of his arms.

"Mind tossing another log on the fire?" Patience asked. "I just got comfortable."

"No problem."

"Thanks."

She watched how he moved away from the door— deliberate, with control, even a certain grace. He seemed attuned to his body, aware of himself in an intriguing way that seemed to just skirt arrogance. Patience hoped she'd quickly get used to having him around. She wanted to relax while she was in New York, concentrate on getting some work done, think of how she might help Tilly. Noticing how Jake Farr moved wasn't conducive to anything constructive.

Bending down, he pulled a neat, clean, New York City-type log from the brass woodbin and set it—he didn't toss it as she would have—on the hot coals.

"I chopped that wood myself," she told him. "Had to clean it up before Terrence would let it in his apartment. Brought almost half a cord down in my Jeep. Tilly knows how to chop wood but doesn't do it anymore. What about you?"

He glanced back at her. "I don't have a working fireplace, but I can manage."

"I have a wood stove myself. Better heat distribution."

"So I've heard." Staying close to the fire, he turned back toward her and settled his eyes deliberately on hers. "I was going to offer to take you out to dinner."

"Dinner? It's almost nine o'clock. I ate hours ago. Made myself an omelet and a salad—there are some eggs in the fridge if you want something to eat. I thought I might make some popcorn in a minute. Don't you New Yorkers get indigestion eating so late?"

"Some of us stay up late, too."

Patience shrugged. She'd already talked too much, chattering on like someone who hadn't seen a human being in months. Well, it had been a few weeks. She'd been finishing up a long, difficult project and hadn't gotten out except for groceries. But yammering on to Jake Farr—well, it was worse than when she'd caught herself talking once too often to Uncle Isaiah's moose head.

"What about a nightcap?" he suggested.

"You mean go out?"

"Sure."

She narrowed her eyes at him, wondering what he was up to. "Why?"

"Because it's a nice evening," he said smoothly, "and I thought you might like to see New York."

"I've seen New York," she said, still suspicious of his motives.

"You come down often? I'm surprised we haven't met—"

"No, I don't come down often, but New York is—well, how often does one have to see it? Big tall buildings are big tall buildings. They're not like trees, you know. Anyway, you shouldn't be surprised we haven't met the few times I have been to the city, because Terrence and I don't exactly get along. I think he'd like to keep me stuffed in a closet when I'm in town."

Jake didn't argue with her nor did he ask her to elaborate. He just looked at her as if he could well understand his friend's attitude.

"Forget the drink," he said, biting back what seemed to her a rather exasperated sigh. "I'll see what I can scrounge up in the kitchen."

Tired as he was, her dog creaked to his feet and followed Jake Farr. Starved for male companionship, Patience decided. Pretty Aphrodite began to purr loudly in her lap, obviously delighted to have Jake— maybe both Jakes—gone.

"I wish I had your sense," Patience muttered.

She was inordinately glad to have Jake Farr back.

She read three pages of *The Three Musketeers* before she realized she hadn't comprehended a single word. She knew why: Jake Farr. He'd shattered her concentration. Annoyed with herself, she flipped back to where she'd started and resumed reading. She couldn't let her imagination get carried away with her.

But she could hear him whistling old rock tunes in the kitchen, and suddenly D'Artagnan and his heroics seemed long ago and very far away.

The two Jakes returned to the library, the two-legged one carrying two beers and a big stainless steel bowl of popcorn. He'd pushed up the sleeves of his black cotton-knit sweater and looked casual, at ease, not as if his heart was thumping madly like hers was. He sat cross-legged on the rug next to the couch and set the bowl on an antique Shaker candlestick table. The dog flopped down beside him.

"I suppose he likes popcorn?" he asked.

"Even more than beer. Is it buttered?"

"Lightly buttered and salted. Otherwise I'd just as soon sit down to a bowl of foam chips. You object?"

"No, I'm on vacation. Besides, I wouldn't want to be an ingrate. Thank you."

"You're welcome." He popped a handful of buttery kernels in his mouth. "What'd you do today?"

"Nothing much."

She reached for a handful of popcorn and noticed he was watching her as if he knew something about her she herself didn't know. That didn't surprise her. She could just imagine what tales Terrence had told him about his sister-in-law. And even Tilly. Being among the Terwilligers and their crowd had given her sister a new twist on the Madrid family. "Patience," she'd said not long ago, "we didn't grow up in a normal family." As if that was news to her. But what was normal? Theirs had been a happy childhood. By Patience's yardstick, that was no mean accomplishment.

"What're you reading?" Jake asked.

She showed him.

"I haven't read that in years."

"Me neither. It hasn't changed though. I never could figure out why it wasn't called *The Four Musketeers*. Porthos, Athos, Aramis and D'Artagnan make four."

"But D'Artagnan was a newcomer."

"True."

Jake tossed a few kernels of popcorn to the other side of the room to lure the dog away from him, but the animal quickly retrieved them and then returned to lay his head on his new friend's lap. It wasn't just the popcorn, Patience knew. Her stupid mutt actually seemed to like Jake Farr, oblivious to the fact that the man clearly wasn't a dog person. Aphrodite blinked up at Patience as if annoyed at these two male interlopers. With a regal yawn, she rose up on all fours, stretched dramatically and jumped off the couch, well clear of the two Jakes. She sauntered off, apparently miffed at having her evening disturbed. Apollo, more of a dope despite his beauty, stayed where he was. Jake didn't comment, but his expression strongly suggested he thought even less of cats—or at least Persian cats—than he did of dogs.

Patience reached for another handful of popcorn. His idea of "lightly" buttered and salted and hers were completely different, but she wasn't about to complain. "Mind if I ask you a question?"

"Not at all."

"Who are you? I know you're Terrence's friend and that your apartment's being redone, but that's about it. If we're going to be roommates, I figure I ought to know a little more about you. I'm not trying to be nosy—"

"That's okay. I'd like to know more about you, too."

Despite how relaxed and casual he looked munching popcorn, Patience observed that his brown eyes were leveled steadily at her, noticing everything. She felt a warm finger of awareness curl up her spine. She resisted it. *Tried* to dismiss it. She was coming off a long winter, and this kind of abrupt, intense physical reaction to virtually the first man she'd seen in months was to be expected. It had nothing, really, to do with Jake Farr himself.

"I own a small consulting business here in New York," he said casually. "JPF Enterprises."

"What's the JPF stand for?"

"Jake Putnam Farr."

As names went, it was almost as elite as Terrence Terwilliger III. "Are you a junior or a third or a fourth or something?"

"No. My parents just liked the name Jake."

"What about Putnam? They didn't just like that, did they?"

He smiled. "My maternal grandmother was a Putnam. How did your parents come up with Matilda and Patience for names?"

"We've never received a straight answer from them on the subject. Mother insists she bought a book of baby names at the grocery checkout and she and Dad each picked a page number and chose the first names they saw. Dad says it was Uncle Isaiah's doing. He was my father's uncle—Tilly's and my great-uncle. According to Dad, he named us after a couple of coonhounds he had. But I don't believe either story."

There she'd gone again, babbling. She could go days without uttering a whole sentence, but not, apparently, around Jake Farr. He didn't seem totally bored, more like bemused. "Your parents and Uncle Isaiah sound . . . interesting."

She laughed. "Oh, they are. Or were, in Uncle Isaiah's case. He died three years ago. I still miss him." But how had they gotten onto the subject of her and her life when what she wanted to know was about him and his life? "So what do people consult JPF on?"

"Management and leadership problems, mostly in small to medium-sized companies."

"You work long hours?"

"I used to. These days I leave more to my staff. You're a nature writer, aren't you?"

Back to her again. Or was he just being polite? She nodded. "I'm a contributing editor to a natural science magazine of minuscule circulation, and I freelance for a number of other magazines, plus script the occasional documentary, teach the odd community-college journalism course. I've also got a couple of nonfiction books on the environment in the works. I just sold a series for elementary kids on living and working in the woods. It's designed to get them thinking about the natural world around them and also to write about it. I've designed various workbooks to go along with it and—" She caught herself again. "But you're supposed to be telling me about yourself, not listening to me go on."

He shrugged. "There's not much more to tell. I'm thirty-eight, I graduated from New York University, I've never been married, I have an apartment on the

Upper West Side and I have parents, a brother, a sister, two nieces and one nephew, all of whom live within an hour's drive of New York."

City birds. Patience grabbed another handful of popcorn, knowing she'd make herself sick if she didn't stop soon.

"You live in the Adirondacks?" he asked.

"Southern Adirondacks, in Uncle Isaiah's old cabin. It's a great place to be a writer."

"Matilda—Tilly—said it was on a lake."

Her mouth full of popcorn, Patience nodded.

"And a ways from the nearest town."

"By Tilly's account, yes. Anything over an hour from the nearest department store she now considers to be in the boonies. But since I hate to shop, that doesn't worry me."

"What do you like to do?"

"Hike, swim, canoe, bird-watch, garden, sew. I've just taken up woodworking. And I read a lot. You?"

"Well, I don't sew," he said, stretching out his long legs, "except for the odd button. And I don't do any woodworking, but the other pastimes you named I do when I've had the chance."

"But what do you do in the city?"

"I enjoy sports, the theater, concerts, and I eat out a lot, like most New Yorkers. Your life seems very solitary."

He seemed more interested in getting her to talk than in talking himself. Behind him, the fire crackled, the glow of its flames seeming to make Jake Farr's eyes darker, mesmerizing. It was quiet in the apartment, almost as quiet as at her mountain cabin. She envisioned him sitting in front of the wood stove in her front room and felt suddenly warm—and a little frightened at her reaction to this man.

She struggled to keep her voice light. "Well, I'm thirty-two and not married. I do have friends and family, but I'm content with my own company. You've been listening to Tilly, haven't you? She thinks I'm another Uncle Isaiah."

"A quasi-hermit, I think is what she said."

"That's because I eat granola and bake my own bread. She should know better. Uncle Isaiah didn't even own a car. Tilly just wants to affirm her own life by comparing mine negatively to hers."

"You two are close?"

"We always have been. We're very direct with each other."

Jake nodded, obviously not surprised. "I can't imagine your being anything but direct. But living alone has to take its toll, especially during a long winter. It must feel good to be in the city."

Diplomatically, Patience withheld comment.

"Look, I don't have a heavy schedule this week. Why don't I show you around?"

"You don't have to—"

"It'd be my pleasure." He gently shoved his canine friend's head off his lap and climbed smoothly to his feet. "Might as well take advantage, Patience. You can sit by a fire reading *The Three Musketeers* in the mountains. And—" he glanced at the sleeping dog "—Jake will get along without you for a few hours."

Patience noticed her throat was dry, her hands clammy. She'd rather have faced a rabid wolf on her doorstep than Jake Putnam Farr offering to show her around town. It wasn't *him* who worried her. It was herself. She needed time to come down off her deadlines and long winter of work before she let a man like this one near her life.

"Thank you for the offer," she said politely, "but, frankly, I don't know what there is to do in the city."

"Then I'll just have to show you the possibilities."

His voice was low and deep, filled with promise and humor, and before she could think of a response, he disappeared down the hall, leaving Patience with a hot finger of awareness trailing slowly, erotically, down her back.

5

As THEY STOOD IN LINE at Zabar's, the one-of-a-kind deli on Broadway, it occurred to Jake that Patience Madrid just might be able to beat him in a fistfight.

He grinned at the thought. She looked fit in black ski pants, a heavy ivory-colored chenille sweater and scarred mud boots with frayed laces. She'd hung a multi-colored chenille scarf around her neck, and whenever the wind blew cold off the Hudson River, she'd pull it up around her ears. Even if she did look as if she ought to have an ax strapped to her back, it was a sexy gesture.

"Nice scarf," he commented.

"Thank you." Her teal eyes fastened on him; she had a directness he found captivating. "A friend of mine wove it."

He should have figured.

Whatever else the woman was, she did not seem to him even the slightest bit depressed. They'd spent the entire morning together, so he thought he'd have noticed. She was stubborn and irascible, just as Terrence had promised, but not even remotely what Jake would call depressed. Had Matilda simply been mistaken about her sister? Or was something else going on?

And, more to the point, was it any of Jake's business?

They paid for their cups of fresh-brewed coffee, and Patience handed Jake his. He noticed her long, slender fingers, the short but manicured nails. There was a small scar below her thumb joint. He couldn't see any noticeable calluses.

"How much further?" she asked when they went back out to the wide, crowded, noisy sidewalk.

"To where?"

She gave him a suspicious look. "To wherever it is we're going."

There was just no use. With anyone else, Jake would have explained—wouldn't have *had* to explain—that they had no destination. They were just walking around the Upper West Side, seeing the sights, getting a feel for the neighborhood. But Patience Madrid wasn't anyone else. If he was uncertain on other points, on that Jake was crystal clear.

His largest point of confusion was why he was so searingly attracted to the woman. God knew it wasn't her boots. And as big and black-lashed and gorgeously teal-blue her eyes were, they weren't the first pair of beautiful eyes he'd seen. The sunlight did have a way of catching the blond highlights in her strawberry hair, and her body, draped in mountain clothes as it was, did have a luscious appeal. But they weren't enough to draw him as inexorably as he was drawn to a woman who didn't like New York, who was argumentative and eccentric, who, for the love of God, dressed like Paul Bunyan.

What was enough, he suspected, was her laugh. It really did have him by the short hairs. Bold and unrestrained, it made him shudder with the pain and mystery of wanting a woman he had no business wanting. His best friend's sister-in-law. A woman committed to a solitary life in the mountains.

Patience Madrid would be an enormous challenge for any man.

"Well?" she prodded. "We *are* going somewhere, aren't we?"

A goal-oriented woman. Jake had no real agenda. He'd just been showing her around.

"My apartment's just a couple of blocks from here," he said quickly. "I thought you might like to see the renovations."

It was lame, and Patience Madrid seemed to know it. "Sounds fine," she said coolly.

But he saw the spots of color high on her peachy cheeks. It wasn't the cold March wind this time. *So,* he thought, *she's not oblivious to what's going on between us.* Jake took heart, even as he warned himself that if she *was* depressed, he'd better be careful with her emotions. Go easy.

"Let's hope the work crew doesn't kick us out."

She seemed to relax slightly, and Jake wondered if it was because they wouldn't be alone. Yet hadn't they been alone together the last two nights? But that was different. At the Terwilligers', they were on neutral ground. Now they were going to be on his turf.

He turned down West 82nd Street toward the Hudson, then cut up West End Avenue. The wind was brisk and cold, even for unpredictable March. The odd daffodil seemed ready to collapse. Not Patience Madrid, however. They'd been on their feet for two hours, and she seemed as fresh as when they'd started out.

Could she beat him in a fistfight? He grinned thoughtfully.

They came to his corner building, its graceful lines a dead giveaway, his architect had told him, of its twenties construction. Jake had bought his apartment for its airiness, its size and its convenient location. He hadn't even thought about its ambience.

Patience tilted her head back and looked all the way up to the top of the fourteen-story building. "Well," she said, "it's not as ostentatious as Tilly's building."

From her, that was a compliment. Jake led her inside, where he introduced her to the doormen and to a neighbor coming through the lobby with two kids and a dog. Patience got down on one knee and let the cocker spaniel lap her face. She and the kids discussed dog bones and flea remedies. Stephen, the father, eyed Jake. "You didn't find her in New York, did you?"

"Not hardly."

"On one of your mountain-climbing expeditions?"

"She's the sister-in-law of a friend of mine."

Stephen nodded, dubious. "Have fun." He gathered up kids and dog and continued on his way.

"Not bad," Patience said, coming up beside Jake. "It always amazes me that normal people live in New York."

Jake let that one slide. Despite his own misgivings about Matilda and Terrence's assessment of Patience's mental state, he supposed a depressed person might have difficulty seeing the good in anything. He couldn't tell if Patience really believed what she was saying or if she was deliberately trying to goad him. Whatever the case, he'd already decided that however this little adventure ended, the Terwilligers owed him one hell of a huge favor. Cheering up Patience Madrid—particularly when she didn't look in need of it—was no easy task. She seemed to enjoy being curmudgeonly.

They took the elevator up to his apartment. It was still covered in dropcloths, the furniture had been moved around or put in storage and carpenters were everywhere doing their thing. Patience visibly relaxed. She started up conversations with various carpenters, inspected their work, made knowledgable comments. One volunteered to take her on a grand tour. She accepted and Jake tagged along. He listened to her discuss plaster, studs, wiring, the virtues of twenties construction. Was it the ski pants, Jake wondered, or the mud boots that made the carpenters take her seriously? Or maybe they were being chivalrous. Humoring her. But when she inquired about kinds of paint and painting procedures, they answered respectfully. It occurred to Jake that no one would humor Patience Madrid.

"It's a great apartment," she told Jake when she'd finished her tour. A carpenter had invited her to have lunch with them, but she'd declined. "You and Terrence have such different tastes. You don't plan to fill up the place with Oriental rugs and priceless urns, do you?"

"They're not my style. Actually, I haven't spent a great deal of time here in the last year."

Her brow furrowed. "Girlfriend?"

"Travels."

"Oh." Was that relief he saw flicker in her eyes? "Well, seeing all these folks working has made me hungry. Is there a decent restaurant around that won't break the bank?"

"One or two," he said, not too sarcastically. "Allow me to treat you."

She didn't even hesitate. "Great. Thanks."

What, he wondered, to make of the woman?

They walked back over to Broadway to a casual, popular restaurant that served great soups and hamburgers, where Patience, in her ski pants and mud boots, wouldn't be out of place. New York, in fact, was a tough city for anyone to stick out in, even a woodswoman. Jake hoped that by the end of her visit she'd see that. Or at least have had a good time.

Maybe I should just hope we both survive.

She ordered Manhattan clam chowder and a hamburger with nothing on it but raw onions. Jake ordered the chowder and the pasta with calamari.

"You eat squid?" she asked.

"On occasion."

"I'd just as soon sit down to a plate full of rubber bands."

"Are you always so open about your opinions?"

"It's just food," she said, not defensively. "You're welcome to eat whatever you like. It's not like I'm criticizing you or your morals or anything important."

"But you don't acquiesce," he said, "just to avoid conflict."

She frowned. "What do you mean?"

"I mean," he went on carefully, "that some people tend to regard disagreement as a sign of disapproval. They're afraid, for example, that if they say they don't like squid the other person might not like them."

Their cups of steaming chowder arrived, with a brimming bowl of oyster crackers. Patience dumped two large spoonfuls into her soup and added a generous grinding of fresh pepper. She popped a cracker into her mouth and regarded Jake thoughtfully. "I can't imagine why anyone would care if I didn't like squid and he did."

"What about a movie?"

"You mean, if you told me you liked such-and-such a movie and I didn't? Well, I guess I'd say so."

Jake didn't "guess"—he *knew* she'd say so. "And a book?"

"Sure. Why not?"

He tried his chowder. It was very hot, loaded with fresh, not canned, clams. "Okay, what about something more personal—say, if I'd made a special dinner for you and served calamari. Would you tell me you'd just as soon eat rubber bands?"

She shook her head. "That'd be rude."

"Would you eat the calamari?"

"I'd choke a little of it down to be polite."

"Suppose I asked you if you liked calamari?"

"Depends how we got along and whether or not I felt you really wanted to know, really cared what I liked and didn't like. In my case, if I made a friend something for dinner that they hated, I'd hope they'd speak up so I could throw on a hot dog or something. If I cared about them, I'd care what they really thought. But there are times—and I think this is what you're getting at—when the social lie is preferable to the truth."

"But generally you speak your mind," Jake said.

"Generally I do."

His pasta with calamari and her hamburger arrived, and he watched her grind what seemed like two pounds of pepper atop her onions, then add a coating of ketchup. "Well," she challenged, "does this gross you out?"

He smiled. "Not at all."

She smiled back. "Is that the truth or a social lie?"

"It's the truth," he said, and it was.

"I believe in tolerance, you know. I just don't believe it means people always have to agree on everything. We don't. And in my opinion, that's not what tolerance means. You like the city, I like the mountains. That doesn't mean the city's an evil place or the mountains are, well, I don't know what."

"Evil, too?"

She shook her head, but seemed to have difficulty holding back a grin. "Nobody could ever think the mountains were evil."

"You are," he said, "an opinionated woman."

"But tolerant."

"What would you like to do this afternoon?"

She re-covered her hamburger and picked the thing up with both hands. "I don't know. What is there to do? I can always go back to Tilly's and work."

As if there were nothing interesting to do in New York. But she was challenging him, Jake decided, throwing down the proverbial gauntlet, saying to him, "Show me something in this town I actually like."

He *had* promised Terrence. *And this is only our first day together.* Refusing to let her draw him into a heated defense of his city, he suggested they go the Museum of Natural History.

She grinned, surprising him. "Now you're talking."

"I'm determined to find something in this city you actually like," he said, just to let her know he was onto her.

"I don't know," she said, "the hamburgers are pretty good. 'Course, it's hard to mess up a burger."

"Patience—"

She laughed. "Got you, Mr. Farr. You should have seen Tilly and me in the old days when Uncle Isaiah was alive—he'd disagree with us just to liven up the conversation. How's the calamari?"

"Tasty."

"To each his own."

The air was warmer and the wind had died down when they headed over to West 79th and the Museum of Natural History, Patience commenting on every crocus and daffodil she saw. She was an observant woman, which Jake admired. But would someone suffering from depression be as aware of the world around her? He had his doubts, more and more convinced that Terrence and Matilda had misread Patience.

The planetarium was her idea. It was empty, very dark, hypnotic. Jake could smell the clean scent of Patience's soap and make out the silhouette of her angular face as the stars shone above them. They might have been on an isolated mountaintop. He fought an urge to kiss her. It was there, as unexpected and undeniable and surprising as a shooting star.

He paid no attention whatsoever to the program.

Patience leaned close to him and whispered, "I love the stars."

Her soft voice, the slight pressure of her shoulder against his, the silhouette of her mass of curls—it was more than Jake could handle. He stared at her instead of the stars.

"You should go star-gazing in the Adirondacks sometime," she said.

He heard the catch in her voice and knew, in his gut, she was thinking what he was thinking, wanting what he was wanting. She could have turned back around in her seat, but didn't. And neither did he. Raising one hand, he touched his fingertips to her lips. Then, before he could talk himself out of it, followed with his mouth. They might have been alone on an Adirondack mountaintop. Her lips seemed to taste of a cool, clear, nothern lake, tempting and startlingly erotic.

This is madness! How could anything feel so right and yet so wrong? "Patience...." And he made himself pull back, hot and tortured because their kiss had been too brief, too slow, too gentle. He wanted more. He wanted, he thought, everything.

What he needed was a good dip in an Adirondack lake.

When the lights came on, Jake waited for her to say something about what had just happened between them, but Patience was quiet, not looking at him. Thinking? Falling into a state of depression? Jake tensed, waiting, hoping he hadn't been totally stupid.

Then she looked around at him and grinned broadly. "Let's go check out the dinosaur bones."

The woman was definitely hard to figure. If Terrence and Matilda had made a mistake about her, Jake could well understand how.

"Sounds good," he told her, and followed her out of the planetarium in search of tyrannosaurus rex.

ALTHOUGH SHE COULD feel her life—or at least her stay in New York—spinning out of control, Patience found herself rummaging in her sister's massive closet. Tilly owned more clothes than Patience had probably bought in her entire life. Most of them wouldn't fit. Tilly was too short and too skinny. There was a black Lycra dress that would stretch to form to Patience's taller, more athletic figure, but she'd just as soon wear black electrician's tape. And she was restricted in terms of shoes: she'd slipped a pair of black suede flats into her suitcase with her sneakers and boots, just in case. She would not fit into any of Tilly's dozens of pairs of size-six shoes.

Scarves, she thought. Maybe she could dress up her black stirrups with a nice scarf.

Or just tell Jake Farr she'd rather eat in tonight. On second thought, being alone with him wasn't such a great idea. He'd invited her to dinner. She'd gotten the distinct impression he didn't think she had anything to wear. Of course, she didn't. It wasn't because she didn't own any dresses that would do for a night out in New York City. It was because she hadn't brought

any with her. She'd expected to spend her sojourn in
the big city holed up in Tilly's apartment with two cats
and a dog and her work. She hadn't expected Jake
Putnam Farr.

She refused to think about their kiss in the planetarium. Absolutely refused.

Tilly had to have *something* Patience could pass off
as her own. Would that be a social lie, she wondered,
or a bald-faced lie? Neither, she decided. Just an ex-
pedient deception. She didn't like it when people assumed she didn't know how to dress just because she
lived up north.

Mercifully, the telephone rang.

"Patience," Tilly said, "I forgot to tell you—I knew
you were coming and would be too stubborn to bring
anything appropriate to wear, so I bought you an
early birthday present. It's in the Bergdorf Good-
man's bag in my closet."

Patience carried the cordless phone with her to the
closet, where she found the bag. She didn't look inside. "Tilly, I smell a rat."

"What do you mean?"

"To be more precise, I smell a manipulative sister.
Did you put Jake Farr up to coming here and showing
me around?"

"Jake is Terrence's friend," Tilly said, cool as she
always was when guilty. "I hardly know him."

Patience humphed. "I was just hunting for something to wear in your closet because Jake and I are going to dinner, and now you call telling me you bought

me clothes. You *are* up to something, Mrs. Terwilliger."

"You have such a suspicious mind. You should write mystery novels. Jake is having his apartment renovated and Terrence let him stay at our place without telling me about it. It's a simple misunderstanding, as I told you. A miscommunication."

"It's just so coincidental, your calling right when I was opening your scarf drawer for something to wear with my stirrups—"

"It *is* a coincidence, Patience. I was at the pool drinking a margarita when I realized it was getting close to dinnertime in New York and you might have regretted not bringing any decent clothes. So I called."

"I do have decent clothes."

"You know what I mean. Stirrups, Patience? Honestly."

When they'd hung up and Patience dumped out the Bergdorf's bag, she did indeed know what her sister had meant. There was a sleek emerald-green velour dress, matching tights, matching crisscross suede shoes, a multicolored scarf that picked up the emerald, big gold earrings and—Tilly being Tilly—a great headband for her mop of strawberry hair.

Patience dressed, did her face with a mix of her sister's cosmetics and the ones she'd brought and slipped into her shoes. Her hair was pretty much hopeless, but the headband helped. She checked her reflection in Tilly's three-sided mirror.

"Hey, not bad," she said aloud.

Jake the dog had wandered into the dressing room and tried to rub against her, but she forbade him. She had no intention of picking dog hair off her dress all through dinner.

The other Jake, the human one, the one who'd upset her equilibrium all day, was waiting for her in the living room, staring out at the New York skyline. It was already seven o'clock. Usually by now she had the dishes done.

Jake turned, and just his eyebrows conveyed that he hadn't expected her to come out dressed the way she was dressed. When he said, "Let's go," she thought his voice sounded huskier than usual. He had on a dark, conservatively cut suit that made him look at once successful, sophisticated and very, very sexy. Was it him? Or had she just been in the woods too long?

They took a taxi to a small, intimate, elegant Italian restaurant on the Upper East Side. The tables were covered with pale yellow cloths and lit with long white candles. The menu was extensive and appetizing. They examined the wine list together and made their choice, Patience noticing the ridiculous markup in price. For dinner, she ordered fresh lemon sole and he picked an eggplant dish. When their bottle of wine came and the waiter filled their glasses, they toasted with a simple "Cheers."

Finally, Patience couldn't stand it any longer. "Jake, what're you up to?"

He uncovered a basket of steaming bread and offered her a piece. When she did not respond, he pulled a piece off the partially cut loaf and spread it with soft butter. "I'm having dinner with an interesting, attractive writer."

It was a smooth answer. "Did Tilly put you up to taking me out?"

"No."

"Well, something's fishy."

Jake looked at her from across the table, the candlelight flickering in his dark eyes. "How so? You came to New York to cat-sit for your sister, only to find her husband had permitted me to stay while my apartment's being renovated. That doesn't strike me as particularly fishy."

"It doesn't?"

He sighed. "I suppose it's a bit coincidental, but—"

"Then taking me around today was your idea?"

"Yes." But before she could decide if she was relieved or not, he added, "And no."

"So you *have* talked to Tilly."

He shook his head. "To Terrence."

Patience almost dropped her wineglass. "*Terrence?* You mean *he* put you up to this?"

"Not exactly. He said you were depressed and—"

"Depressed? Me? I can't believe . . . I swear that man . . . Well, I won't say it since he's your friend. But look at me, Jake. Do I look depressed?"

Leaning back in his chair, Jake did look at her for longer than she felt he needed to make his assessment, and more closely than she found comfortable. His expression was impossible to read in the shadows. She hoped her reaction, the heat rushing to her cheeks, was also not apparent.

"No," he said finally, "I wouldn't say you look depressed."

Patience struggled to keep her balance, aware of Jake Farr's eyes still on her. "Where'd he ever get such a loony idea?"

Jake didn't answer.

Putting two and two together, Patience said, "Tilly."

Again Jake diplomatically withheld comment.

"What's gotten into her?" Patience muttered, irritated and embarrassed and just plain surprised. Her sister had plunged right off the deep end without her noticing.

"I have no intention of coming between you and your sister."

"Then don't," she snapped, not angry at him so much as disturbed by this new gulf between her and her sister.

"Patience, I asked you to dinner tonight because I wanted to be with you." His voice was calm, reasonable . . . and seductive. "I wanted to get to know you better. I'd already decided Terrence was mistaken about your mental state and—"

"My mental state." She nearly choked. "I really don't appreciate you and my brother-in-law discussing me behind my back."

Jake didn't retreat. "I don't blame you for being upset."

"I am not upset," she said testily. Where was her self-control? "I am *angry,* Jake, and getting angrier by the second. Don't you get it? Tilly has to know I'm not depressed. I don't even understand depression. She just said that because—" She broke off, not wanting to put her foot in her mouth. In her emotional state, she knew she'd say something about herself, her sister, Tilly's marriage. Or she'd say something about how being around Jake Farr all day—and their kiss—had catapulted her senses into overdrive. She'd regret it, whatever she said.

Their dinners arrived, and she smiled at the waiter and said everything was fine, and so did Jake. Then the waiter brought freshly grated pepper and Parmesan cheese, and finally withdrew. Jake refilled their wineglasses, looking unperturbed, controlled. Of course, he wasn't the one having tales told about him.

The fish smelled wonderful. So did Jake's eggplant.

And she was hungry.

"I think I know what's going on," Jake said.

"I thought you might." He was not a stupid man.

Without looking at her, he went on, "Your sister arranged this weekend to get us together."

Bingo.

But Patience didn't say a word. Obviously her sister was trying—consciously or not—to distract herself from her own romantic difficulties. But, as annoyed as she was with Tilly, she refused to confide her sister's most private problems to Terrence's best friend.

"Look," Jake went on, "it's not the first time a friend's done something like this to me, or for me, depending on your point of view."

Patience quickly swallowed some of her wine, wondering if she were just another in a long line of women presented to Jake Farr and rejected by him. The idea didn't sit well with her at all. "If you don't mind," she said coolly, "I need to sort this out in my own mind first. Can we just back-burner this one and enjoy our dinner?"

"That," Jake said, "is a wonderful idea."

And he smiled, a raw, gentle, sensitive, hungry smile that left her ten times as confused as she'd been a moment ago. Should she thank Tilly for putting her and Jake Farr together?

No. Jake had just been decent the past twenty-four hours because he'd thought she was depressed. It was sheer lunacy. The woman he thought he'd been taking around the Upper West Side today—the one he'd seemed attracted to—wasn't her. His actions, his assessment of her, had been colored by having been told she was depressed.

It was just too much. But what was she going to do about it?

Enjoy dinner, she thought. And deal with Tilly Terwilliger the first chance she got.

"YES, I'M SURE I have the name right. The Hidden Camel Resort in Scottsdale, Arizona."

"I'm sorry, ma'am, but there's no listing—"

"There has to be."

"Please check the name and city and try again, ma'am. We'll be glad to assist you."

Patience hung up the phone, frustrated and vaguely worried. Now what? Maybe she just needed to sleep. Look at things fresh in the morning. She'd eaten too much and spent too much time with a certain tall, gorgeous man today. Tomorrow everything would make sense.

Only it wouldn't, and she knew it.

In her stocking feet, she returned to the living room, where her temporary roommate seemed transfixed by the New York skyline. Her breath caught in her throat. He'd taken off his jacket and rolled up the shirt-sleeves. The dark hairs of his arms contrasted with the stark white of the expensive fabric. He seemed pensive and as hard to figure as ever. If only Tilly hadn't stuck her big nose into her life . . .

She might never have gotten around to meeting Jake Farr. And then what? *I wouldn't be feeling so damned out of my element is what.*

"Even my moose head didn't make me this nuts," she muttered.

Jake turned. "I beg your pardon?"

Even as polite as he was, she could hear the huskiness in his voice, the undertone of confusion and irritation. After dinner, they'd taken a taxi back to Central Park West. It must have been a smaller cab than the first one, because Patience didn't remember sitting so close to Jake, feeling his thigh brush up against hers, noticing his hands, his strong chin, the tiny scar at the corner of his right eye. When they arrived at the apartment, she'd fled into her borrowed bedroom to call her sister, hoping whatever had gotten into her in the cab—that shocking, insidious awareness of him—would have gotten out again by the time she had to face him.

It hadn't.

"Nothing," she said. "I can't get hold of Tilly."

"She'll call you back?"

"No, I didn't leave a message."

Technically, she wasn't telling a falsehood; she *hadn't* left a message. But that was only because her rat-fink sister hadn't told her where she was really staying.

"Maybe she and Terrence are still at dinner," Jake suggested. "It's early yet."

Patience didn't disabuse him of his notion that Terrence and Tilly were in Florida together. Until she and Tilly could have a proper heart-to-heart, Patience was unwilling to reveal anything to Terrence's best friend.

Sitting on one of the Terwilligers' elegant couches, Jake asked casually, "Where is the Hidden Flamingo, anyway? I've never heard of it, and I didn't think to ask. I assumed the Orlando area, but—Patience, is something wrong?"

The Hidden Flamingo in Florida.

The Hidden Camel in Arizona.

First, she and Jake Farr had ended up on Central Park West at the same time. Next, Tilly had arranged for Terrence to tell Jake her sister was depressed. But now, the Hidden Flamingo and the Hidden Camel? That was too much for Patience to swallow.

This really was war.

"Patience?"

"I need to think before I tell you more," she said.

She wasn't looking at him, but could feel his eyes boring into her. A curious warmth spread through her. Finally, she gave him a quick glance. Indeed, his eyes were pinned to her. Dark, narrowed, knowing eyes.

"What?" she asked, her tone just this side of demanding.

"I'm just trying to think of a way," he said, "to get you to trust me."

Then he was on his feet, and in two steps was only an inch away. She could smell his cologne and see the stubble of his beard. He studied her face, and she wondered what he could see. Anger? Confusion? Smudged mascara? A woman who desperately wanted to trust him?

He touched the corner of her mouth with his finger briefly, for a fraction of a second. She had no idea why. He didn't explain, she didn't ask. But just that simple breath of a touch ignited the center of her, and she forgot all about her crazy sister's schemes and troubled marriage.

"I trust you," she said, surprised at how certain she sounded. "We've spent the last two nights together, haven't we? I mean, not together-together, which maybe is the whole point . . . oh, hell, you know what I mean."

"I think I do." His voice was still low, seductive. "But I'm not asking if you trust me to be an ordinary, decent human being and not attack you. I'm asking, do you trust me?"

And his lips touched where his finger had, for half a breath longer.

She knew exactly what he was asking.

But he didn't give her a chance to answer. His mouth covered hers, pressing his case. He drew her to him, so that she could feel the hardness of him, as his tongue parted her lips. She responded to his urgency, and to her own.

Jake pulled away and asked again in a hoarse voice. "Do you trust me?"

She nodded, unable to speak.

"Good."

Patience found her voice. "Why is it good?"

"Because—" He paused, holding her, but his expression unreadable. "Because I just spent a day with an intriguing woman who's used to making her own decisions and fighting her own battles. Maybe too used to it. I can say that because I'm like that myself, except maybe not so intriguing."

"I don't know about that. I have more questions about you tonight than I did this morning."

"Ditto me about you." He laughed, a rich, deep, free laugh. "Fun, isn't it?"

"I need to think before I tell you more," she said.

"I'm not trying to make you tell me anything you don't want to tell me. I just want you to feel you can trust me. Terrence is a friend, but so is Matilda... Tilly. And I'd like to think you are, too."

Before she could respond, Jake the dog worked his way between them, rubbing hair on her velour dress and the other Jake's charcoal trousers. He brushed his thigh in disgust.

Patience winced. "I'm sorry—"

He waved off her apology. "I'm flattered he's jealous."

"Actually," she said, "I think he just wants a beer."

Jake laughed. "Then that's two of us."

Feeling strangely unsettled and yet wholly intrigued, Patience watched the two Jakes lope off to the kitchen. When they were out of sight, Apollo and Aphrodite strolled out to greet her, rubbing white hairs against her emerald tights.

Suddenly she knew what she had to do.

Looking out at the New York skyline, the buildings that seemed almost alive with lights against the night sky, she imagined the stars above her cabin, how they'd sparkle on her moonlit lake.

She had to go home. Dog, cats, sister, brother-in-law and attractive New York businessman or not. In the mountains, far away from Jake Putnam Farr, she could think clearly.

On her way to bed, she could hear Jake giving his new canine companion the lowdown on a long list of domestic and imported beers, and she smiled, genuinely liking the man.

Which was as good a reason as any, in her view, to get the hell out of New York.

6

JAKE HEARD PATIENCE fumbling around the apartment, collecting cats and dog, throwing her things together, preparing to make her exit. Folding his hands under his neck, he settled back against the multitude of pillows on the big bed. He debated going out and saying goodbye. But it was six o'clock in the morning and she was deliberately trying to sneak out before he got up.

He'd let her.

There was no good reason for her to be leaving. So what if Matilda had engineered their week together? He'd been the victim of far worse would-be matchmakers. And it wasn't as if he and Patience Madrid hadn't been getting along. They had.

Which no doubt was the real reason for this mad exit. He'd touched a raw nerve and now she was making good her escape.

Or was he being arrogant?

Her departure could also have damned little to do with him. He recalled her reaction to his question about the Hidden Flamingo. Terrence hadn't left a number as he'd promised, otherwise Jake would have called him and demanded to know what in blazes was

going on. But why had Patience looked so shocked
and suspicious when he'd mentioned where her sister
and brother-in-law were staying?

"I need to think before I tell you more."

Well, apparently she'd done her thinking and had
decided *not* to tell him more.

"Jake," she called in a loud whisper. He knew she
didn't mean him. "Jake, no, you can't go in there. Now
come on."

He could hear the dog sniffing at his bedroom door.
He'd miss the ugly hound.

But they'd see each other again soon. Jake was
confident of that. He and Patience Madrid had unfin-
ished business, whether she'd admit it or not.

When he was sure she was gone, he rolled out of bed
and wandered into the kitchen, where he wasn't surprised to find a curt note from his ex-roommate.

Dear Jake,
I decided to return home—I've taken the cats
with me, so you needn't worry about them. I'll
let Tilly know. Help yourself to the groceries I
left.
And thanks for showing me around NYC. It was
more fun than I'd expected.

Patience

It wasn't the sort of note worth keeping for poster-
ity. He crumpled it up and tossed it in the trash can,
only to notice a small heap of crumpled-up notes. He

scooped them out and dumped them on the table, then smoothed them one by one. Each was an aborted attempt at a note to him. There were seven tries in all.

"Dear Jake, Sorry I didn't say goodbye, but I didn't want to wake you."

"Dear Jake, It's been fun, but"

"Dear Jake, I'm sure I must seem a coward to you sneaking off at the crack of dawn, but I wanted to beat rush hour and"

"Jake, Apollo, Aphrodite and I have gone to the mountains. See you. P.M."

"Jake:"

"Jake: Decided to head home, but not on account of you or anything we"

"Dear Jake, I had a great time with you in New York, but decided to head home. Took the animals with me. Enjoy your stay on Central Park West. I'll be in touch. No, I won't."

So. She'd struggled to find the right words for her goodbye note. He was amused. Flattered. *Challenged.*

Where in the Adirondacks did Terrence say his unusual sister-in-law lived?

He found a map of New York, and, over a pot of coffee, scoured the northeast corner of the state for a town, village, mountaintop, route number or lake that sounded familiar.

Patience Madrid hadn't heard the last of him.

SIX HOURS AFTER she'd arrived back at her lakeside cabin, Patience had been for a walk around the lake with Jake, filled her woodbox, lit the stove, made a pot of chili and given up on keeping her visitors from New York fluffy and white. They'd appropriated Jake's spot under the wood stove. He hadn't minded at first; three nights in the big city had given him a taste for human beds. But after Patience kicked him off her bed the third time and threatened to throw him outside for the balance of Apollo and Aphrodite's visit, he decided he wanted back his spot under the stove. The cats, however, wouldn't budge. It didn't seem to occur to any of the three animals that Jake was big enough to insist.

Leaving well enough alone, Patience curled up on her sofa with a notepad for a brainstorming session. Nothing like work to ease one's mind.

She wondered what Jake Farr had done when he'd found her note. For a while she'd entertained the fantasy—a word she never thought she'd associate with her feet-flat-on-the-floor self—that he'd immediately set out for the Adirondacks. But he'd have been here by now. Unless he'd gotten lost....

"Nope," she said aloud, "he's not the type to get lost."

So what had he done?

Tossed out her note, eaten breakfast and gotten on with his life.

She sighed, and then the telephone rang.

Tilly was in a rage. "Patience, I don't believe you. You have Apollo and Aphrodite in the *mountains!*"

It wasn't a question. Obviously Tilly already knew the answer. It was more an expression of outrage and incredulity. Nevertheless, Patience reined in her own annoyance and said, "Sure. They're having a ball."

"Doing what?"

Patience didn't appreciate the unrepentant note of suspicion in her sister's voice. "Enjoying life in the beautiful Adirondacks."

"You haven't let them outside, have you?"

"No, of course not." She'd tried; they wouldn't go. Nothing irritated her more than house cats. "Tilly, quit worrying. You know I'd never let anything happen to them."

"They're not country cats."

This was not news to Patience.

Tilly groaned. "I wish you'd told me you were taking them up to the cabin with you."

"I would have," Patience said coolly, "but I didn't have your number."

"Yes, I know."

Again, not even a hint of guilt. "How did you know I was here?"

"How do you think? Jake Farr told me when I tried to reach you a little while ago."

Patience licked her lips. She didn't want to give away her confused feelings toward her brother-in-law's best friend. Coming home hadn't put him out of her mind, as she'd hoped. "Then he's staying on at your apartment?"

"For now." Tilly paused, then cleared her throat. "How much does he know?"

"Nothing."

"How'd you find me out?"

"The Hidden Camel and the Hidden Flamingo, Til? Come on, you could have done better."

"So I'm not a writer like you."

"I deal in nonfiction, Tilly. Facts, not make-believe, not *lies*. The hurting marriage, the separate vacations—all a ruse to get me and Jake Farr together?"

There was a silence on the other end—wherever it was—of the phone.

Then Tilly said softly, "Not entirely."

Patience felt a knife-stab of guilt. "You want to tell me what really is going on?"

"I can't."

"Can't or won't?"

"A little of both. I don't mean to be closemouthed, Patience, but I'm in an awkward position. I'll tell you everything when I get back. I promise."

"What about Terrence?"

"He's still my husband," Tilly said vaguely and, Patience thought, a little desperately.

"I'll tend Apollo and Aphrodite," Patience said. "Don't worry about them, okay?"

"What about Jake?"

"Well, if the cats give him his place back under the stove I think they'll get along well."

Tilly gave a small hiss of pure, sisterly irritation. "I didn't mean your confounded dog, Patience. I meant Jake Farr."

"Oh."

"When I spoke with him, he sounded, I don't know, not annoyed with you, really. Just determined."

"Determined to do what?"

"I couldn't say."

Apollo slithered out from under the wood stove, stretched and hopped onto Patience's lap. He was covered with soot, sawdust and wood chips. Nothing like a white cat to point out one's housekeeping deficiencies.

"Well," Patience said, "it doesn't matter. He's in New York and I'm up here at the lake. By the way, was my being depressed your idea or Terrence's?"

"Your being what?"

"Depressed, Tilly. Don't act as if you don't know. Terrence told his pal Jake that his weird sister-in-law was depressed and could he please show her around New York."

"Are you serious? Patience, you've never been depressed in your life. It's just not your style."

"I know that," she snapped, really confused now.

Tilly sighed. "No, telling Jake you were depressed was not my idea."

"Look, you and Terrence just get your act together where I'm concerned, okay? I don't need you messing around in my life."

"I understand. Really I do. But . . . you can't blame Terrence for thinking—if it is what he thought—that Jake was your type, can you?"

"How can a New York businessman be my type?"

"It's not as if he's an ordinary New York business-man. Good Lord, Patience, Jake Farr's climbed more mountains than you have!"

And on that note Tilly said goodbye and hung up without mentioning where she was staying or what, exactly, she and Terrence were up to. Patience resisted the urge to throw her phone across the room.

Why did she feel as if the heavy hand of fate had given her life a good swat?

She patted Apollo, and he immediately began to purr. Jake had wormed his way underneath the stove, and Aphrodite, as filthy as her fellow Persian, had curled up on his stomach.

"Good Lord, Patience, Jake Farr's climbed more mountains than you have!"

"Well," she said aloud, "I've never claimed to be a terrific judge of people."

Male people in particular.

Had she misjudged Jake Putnam Farr?

No, she thought. She hadn't misjudged him. She hadn't judged him at all. She'd fled New York before she'd given herself that chance.

"So, what next?"

A good night's sleep. Cabin-scrubbing in the morning. Then baths for cats and maybe Jake as well.

There was nothing like physical labor and fresh mountain air to stimulate the brain. By tomorrow afternoon, she'd have a plan of action to figure out what to do about her sister, her brother-in-law and the mountain-climbing New York businessman.

Jake Farr wasn't the only one who knew how to be determined.

IT WAS DARKER than the pits of hell at midnight in the Adirondack Mountains.

Jake crept along the narrow dirt road in his Acura, grateful he didn't go for low-slung sports cars. As it was, he'd gone into a few potholes he'd thought he'd never come out of again. Matilda had warned him.

"It's a rough road," she'd said. "Patience loses her muffler every spring."

He'd thought Tilly had been exaggerating.

He hoped to hell he had the right dirt road.

"It winds around through the woods for a mile or so before you come to the lake, which kind of sneaks up on you."

Seeing how the Adirondack State Park was six million acres' worth of forest, Jake had had no trouble finding a dirt road through the woods. And there were thousands of lakes. Chances were this dirt road, even if the wrong one, would land him on the shores of a lake.

A furry creature scurried in front of his car. Jake could see bright eyes reflected in his headlights and a black silhouette that was too big for a raccoon and too small for a bear. It disappeared into the woods, and he didn't contemplate what species it might be. He checked his gas tank. Half-full. He hadn't thought to pack any camping gear in the trunk. What if he didn't come upon the Madrid cabin soon? What if he had to spend the night out in the wilderness? He'd survive, of course. He knew his way around the woods. But he doubted he'd be in any temper to deal with Miss Patience Madrid in the morning.

"Trust me," her sister had said, "she lives *way* out in the woods."

He hadn't seen any evidence of human habitation since the exit off the interstate, over forty minutes ago.

What had he gotten himself into this time?

"I wouldn't ask this of you, Jake, but I'm really worried about my sister."

Yes, yes. And what a good soul he was to drag himself off to the wilderness to find her. He'd had tickets to the Rangers game that evening. Behind the penalty box.

Why didn't the Patience Madrid he'd kissed and the Patience Madrid her sister described not jive? Those two Patiences were why he'd headed north. He had to reconcile them. He had to know who he'd kissed last night, who he'd dreamed about, who he couldn't get out of his mind. He had to find out who Terrence's strawberry-haired sister-in-law was and whether or not he should leave her in the woods with her animals.

"Holy—"

He crashed on his brakes and came to a screeching halt inches, it seemed, from a glass-still lake. His heart pounding, he sat with his foot hard on the brake and stared across the quiet waters that reflected the star-dotted night sky. He loosened his grip on the steering wheel. Swallowed. Breathed again.

He was here, in Madrid country. And it was as startlingly beautiful, as eerily seductive as he ever could have imagined. If he were going to be a hermit, he should be so lucky to pick a spot as breathtaking as this one.

"Make a ninety-degree turn to the right," Tilly Terwilliger had directed. "Follow the road all the way around to the other side of the lake. You'll go past a couple of summer cabins. Patience's will be the last one you come to—she has the whole north side of the lake to herself. If it's cold, it'll probably have smoke coming out of the chimney."

Following her sister's instructions, Jake backed up and made the turn. If possible, the road narrowed even more. There were ruts, rocks, holes, the odd branch, more scurrying creatures. A lovely cabin with a huge deck on his left. A steep incline, then another cabin. Both were deserted for the winter. The road veered off into the woods again, away from the lake, and after another half mile there was another cabin, this one older, less attractive. He bounced through three holes in quick succession. He thought his muffler was gone for sure, but it held fast.

What did Patience do when she ran out of milk?

How had he let Tilly talk him into this escapade?

She didn't. You'd already decided to go. She just gave you an excuse.

"Madness," he said, negotiating a steep downhill turn.

Once more, through the dark silhouettes of the tall evergreens, he could see the starlit mirror of the lake. He had to be getting close.

Then an old log cabin came into view, nestled into the woods not far from shore. A dim light burned somewhere inside. And smoke was, indeed, curling from the stone chimney. Jake turned into the narrow driveway and parked, debating for a few seconds before turning off his engine whether or not to head back to New York. Patience had sneaked out on him that morning. Maybe it had been a difficult decision, but she'd made it, stuck to it. What right did he have barging in on her? Hadn't she denied being even remotely depressed?

"Of course she denied it!" Tilly had groaned. "Patience would never admit a weakness."

So, Jake thought, he'd made *his* difficult decision. And now he had to stick to it.

He shut off his car engine and climbed out, the crisp, cold Adirondack air instantly reinvigorating him. He grabbed his knapsack from the back seat, slung it over one shoulder and started along a flagstone path to the front of the cabin. He moved with care. If Jake were an outdoor dog, he might not recognize him right away and attack. Or there could be other nocturnal creatures lurking about.

In any case, he was definitely in Madrid country and prepared for anything.

He felt only slightly guilty about showing up on Patience's doorstep in the middle of the night. After all, within the past few days he'd been accosted by her dog in an elevator and had his bed confiscated by her and her creatures.

He climbed up onto the porch and knocked on her solid, rough-wood door. "Patience?"

"It's a good thing," her voice said behind him, "that I look before I shoot."

He turned slowly, carefully, and sure enough, there she stood behind him in a red union suit, her hair sticking out everywhere, pointing a shotgun at him.

"Your teeth are chattering," he said.

She lowered her gun. "Wouldn't affect my aim."

"Hello, Patience."

"Hello, Jake."

"Mind if I come in?"

She didn't answer right away. "Door's open. Don't let the cats out."

He went inside, and she followed, shutting the door hard behind her. She leaned her shotgun up against the wall. It looked maybe eighty years old.

"Is it loaded?" he asked.

"Nope. If you'd been a stranger up to no good I'd have just whacked you over the head. I don't need

ammunition to do that. I heard you coming about fifteen minutes ago and snuck outside, just in case."

The contradictions Jake had come to expect from
Patience Madrid were in evidence. The chattering
teeth coupled with the tough talk. The long, slender
fingers and feminine curves under the well-worn,
purely functional union suit. The wild hair framing
the clear, peachy skin and wide, sensitive eyes. She
seemed absolutely, incontrovertibly confident, and,
at the same time, curiously, agonizingly vulnerable.

Jake had never met a woman he wanted to know
more.

She flipped on a copper lamp above a small, round
oak table in what passed for a dining area. As far as
he could tell, her cabin consisted of two cozy, charming rooms. The kitchen, dining and living areas
formed an L. The furnishings were a mix of flea market and hand-crafted pieces. Tilly's two cats and Patience's dog were asleep together under the wood
stove. How they all fit Jake couldn't have said. He
duly noted the state-of-the-art computer and laser
printer on the far wall, under a portrait of an old man
with a white bushy beard standing next to a dog or a
bear, Jake couldn't tell which. The infamous Uncle
Isaiah, he presumed.

Through an open doorway, he caught a peek of an
unmade bed.

"Sorry I woke you," he said.

"I wasn't asleep. Mind telling me what you're doing here?"

In the dim light, he could see the clear teal of her eyes, the stubborn set of her jaw. Patience Madrid didn't trust him. She wasn't afraid of him—she just didn't trust him.

"I spoke to your sister. She's worried about you."

"Horsefeathers."

"It's true. She asked me to check on you."

Patience sighed. "Because I'm depressed?"

"On the verge of becoming a misanthropic hermit. She wouldn't call it depression."

Grumbling, Patience pulled a pitted kettle off the wood stove and, with her free hand, grabbed two mugs from an open shelf. "Tea?" she asked.

"I'd love some."

He almost changed his mind when she dumped a tablespoon of what looked like bird food in each of the mugs. She added water, banged the kettle back down on the stove and threw on another log. Definitely a woman who could fend for herself.

She set the two mugs on the table, next to a stack of newspapers and magazines. Jake pulled out a chair, but didn't sit down right away. Most of whatever Patience had dumped in his cup had settled to the bottom, but a few odd pods and leaves were floating on the surface.

"It's a soothing mixture of herbs," she said. "I forget what all kinds."

"Don't you have a strainer?"

"Somewhere."

But she sat down and sipped at her brew, and Jake decided he'd best make do.

The stuff was dreadful.

"I've been working hard," Patience said, "and I haven't been out much this winter. But I'm not depressed and I'm not a 'misanthropic hermit.' Can't you see what Tilly's doing?"

Truthfully, he couldn't. He'd given up on trying to figure out the Madrid sisters at all. In fact, as certain as he was driving up from New York that he was doing the right thing, now he couldn't imagine how he'd swallowed Matilda Madrid Terwilliger's line. Her sister seemed fine.

"What do *you* think she's doing?" he asked, keeping his calm.

"Trying to keep us together. Physically together. I mean..." She blushed, which, Jake would guess, was an unusual experience for her. "She's matchmaking."

"I see."

"I told you that before."

"Yes, but she insists she can't imagine any two people more unsuited for each other than the two of us, that she's not matchmaking but trying to keep you from becoming another Uncle Isaiah."

Patience looked at him. "Oh."

"I'm at a loss as to whom to believe."

"Well, it's not as if *I* think we're suited for each other...."

He smiled. It clearly had crossed her mind.

Her spine ramrod-straight, she rose, mug in hand. "I'm going to bed. You're welcome to spend the night—the couch is reasonably comfortable. If you need another blanket, give a yell. We'll figure out this mess in the morning."

She crammed another log onto the fire, then headed off to bed, firmly closing the door behind her.

Alone in the L-shaped room, Jake could hear animals breathing, the fire crackling. How the hell had he ended up here? He poured his "tea" down the drain. Through the window above the sink he could see the shadows of the tall evergreens around the cabin, the seemingly endless night. Not even in the distance could he hear the scream of a police or ambulance siren, the honking of taxi horns.

The couch *was* only reasonably comfortable.

He kicked off his shoes but left on his jeans lest God-knew-what disturbed him in the night, then pulled the thick, soft, worn afghan up over him.

Jake the dog crept out from under the wood stove and licked his face, flopping down alongside the couch. He smelled of pine and long-dead leaves. Apollo and Aphrodite, no longer snow-white, peered suspiciously at the two Jakes from under the stove.

All in all, Jake had to admit Patience Madrid didn't have a bad life in the mountains. But what did she do when she tired of four-legged company?

7

PATIENCE WOKE at six o'clock, glad she was in her own bed in her own house. There was no danger, however, of her barging in on Jake Farr in the next room. She had not forgotten he was there.

"Not bloody likely I would," she muttered, throwing back the covers.

She got dressed and crept across her small bedroom. After sharing the Terwilligers' apartment with Mr. New York, she was well aware he didn't keep the same hours she did. She cracked the bedroom door and peered into the front room. All seemed quiet and peaceful. She had no idea how late Jake would sleep. He'd seemed pretty tired last night and wasn't conditioned to early rising the way she was. She'd *tried* to sleep late.

Opening the door a bit wider, she looked left to where the couch was pushed up against the wall. She didn't know how long she could stand being confined to her room. She had things to do.

Jake looked twisted and uncomfortable, one black-stockinged foot poking out from the end of her afghan, his arms at odd angles. His eyes were closed.

Patience noticed the dark shadow of beard on his square, upper-class jaw.

How did Jake Putnam Farr end up asleep on her couch?

"Better than asleep in your bed," she grumbled well under her breath. "Or worse."

He stirred.

"I'm awake," he said, not sounding pleased.

"Awake-awake or getting there?"

"Neither." He still hadn't opened his eyes. "I can't say I've been asleep."

"Rough night?"

"Your dog wanted to go out sometime around five o'clock."

"He's a little off his schedule because of New York. Usually he waits until five-thirty or even six."

"How charming."

"Did you let him out?"

His eyes opened. "I walked him."

She laughed. She couldn't help it.

Jake Farr glared at her. "What the hell's so funny?"

"Well . . ." She tried to control herself. "You don't walk dogs up here. You just open the door and let them go do their thing. You walk dogs in New York."

She went over to the stove, noticing her Jake squished up under it, looking very pleased with himself. Obviously he enjoyed putting one over on a rich New Yorker. Patience tried not to share too much in his amusement; Jake Farr *was* her guest. She noticed it was foggy out. Ahh, March.

Heat—plenty of it—radiated from the stove. Or was it having Jake Farr's eyes on her? She'd put on heavy dark green leggings and an oversize roll-top yellow sweater, a concession to her intensely male guest. Or her reaction to him.

"I kept the fire going," he said.

"Thank you."

"You're welcome, but it was just self-preservation."

He'd sat up, thrown off the afghan. He looked rumpled and about as egregiously sexy as any man had a right to look. He ran one hand through his hair, a gesture Patience found irresistibly masculine. Her physical response to him, from the tingling in her lips right down to her toenails, was way out of bounds. She had to regain some control before she did something she regretted. She knew she could count on her good sense to stop her. But it was that feeling that she'd *like* to do something she'd regret that ate at her.

That and Jake Farr's overwhelming physical presence.

"I'm surprised I didn't hear you," she said. "I must have slept more soundly than I thought."

Soundly, but not easily. She'd had full-color dreams of her and Jake Farr. She refused to analyze them, at least not while he was camped out on her couch. Right now, Jake was too real—too much of a threat to her stability—for her to examine her subconscious thoughts about him.

"Something hot to drink?" she asked.

"Such as?"

He sounded suspicious. Obviously he hadn't liked her tea last night. "Coffee."

She ground some mocha java beans, got out an unbleached filter, dumped in the coffee and poured on boiling water. She flipped on the public radio station broadcast out of Albany and listened to "Morning Edition." Jake emerged from under the stove and she let him out. Then the cats deigned to show their presence, rubbing up against her legs and purring until she finally fed them. No fancy cat dishes in her house. They got a couple of tin plates Uncle Isaiah had left behind.

While she rinsed out the can of cat food for recycling, she sensed Jake's presence behind her. She said idly, "Apollo and Aphrodite are beginning to look like real cats, don't you think?"

"You'll bathe them before you return them to your sister?"

"I suppose I'll have to."

The coffee made, Patience poured two mugs and sliced a couple of bagels she'd brought with her from New York. She placed them in the wood stove oven to heat up, then banged the door shut with her foot. She didn't have any cream cheese, so she put out butter and natural peanut butter. To make room for her company, she piled up her newspapers and magazines and shoved them to one side.

"What did you think you'd accomplish by coming here?" she asked, trying to sound casual, as if she didn't much care.

Jake shrugged. She thought she detected the same level of forced casualness in him. "I don't know."

"Tilly had you worried?"

"Not really. She's the one who was worried. Even if she was exaggerating—"

"She was *lying*, Jake."

He sat down at the table and sipped his coffee before answering. "I couldn't take that chance."

"Why not? It's not as if you owe me anything. We only just met."

"True, but Terrence and your sister are my friends. I felt I owed them at least the effort of looking in on you and reassuring them you were fine."

Patience didn't know whether or not to be insulted, or even just slightly miffed. Did she want Jake Farr to tell her he'd headed north because he wanted to see her again?

She leaped up suddenly and snatched the bagels out of the oven. She'd almost let them burn.

"They're a little crisp," she said, "but they'll do."

Jake was smiling. "You seem at home here."

"I *am* at home here."

"But you seemed just as at home on Central Park West. Cooking on a wood stove or a restaurant-style stove doesn't seem to make much difference to you."

She pointed her knife at her small kitchen area. "I have a regular stove here, too."

It wasn't, however, anything like the Terwilligers' expensive, state-of-the-art stove.

"You don't need to be defensive."

"I'm not."

"I'm merely suggesting that you have the ability to adapt, to make the best of any given situation, that your surroundings—material things—aren't all that important to you."

She laughed. "Good thing, huh?"

"Yes," he said, taking in her modest accommodations, "one could say that."

"What about you?"

"Given a choice between an expensive apartment and a great view, I'll take the view. But it depends on the circumstances."

"Tilly says you like to climb mountains." Of course, Tilly had also adamantly denied having told Jake Farr her sister was depressed.

"It's a hobby of mine, yes."

"What kind of mountains?"

"Virtually any kind. I've done all the peaks in the Adirondacks. In fact, I was supposed to have gone climbing in New Zealand during the renovations on my apartment, but that trip fell through, which is how I ended up at your sister's."

Mountain-climbing in New Zealand. The man did defy expectations. Patience wished she'd spent more time grilling Tilly on Jake Farr's background.

After breakfast, he insisted on cleaning up, and she was happy to let him at her kitchen. Grabbing a jacket, she headed outside. She needed a dose of fresh, cold mountain air to regain her equilibrium.

She'd enjoyed having Jake Farr across her break-fast table. She'd thought too much about rubbing the back of her hand across his stubble of beard. Thought too much about where he might sleep tonight, if he stayed.

What had happened to her peaceful, orderly, pro-ductive life?

She headed down to the lake and walked out to the end of the dock, the four-legged Jake at her heels. Morning fog swirled over the water. The air was downright springlike. She inhaled deep lungfuls of it, glad to be home, away from New York and—

"And its excitement," she finished aloud, forcing herself to be honest.

New York City was an energetic place. She remem-bered the glittering skyline outside Tilly's apartment, the rush she'd felt when she'd seen Jake's renova-tions, the elegant dinner they'd had together and how sophisticated she'd felt. Contrary to popular belief, she did enjoy dressing up and going out once in a while. Putting on evening clothes, makeup, panty hose, heels. So she'd been holed up all winter work-ing. Did that mean she was a hermit? It wasn't as if she holed up *every* winter.

Or was it Jake Putnam Farr who had made her see New York in a different light? The man had worked his way under her skin and was hell-bent, it seemed, for her soul. And she didn't know why. *Why* was she so attracted to him?

And was he attracted to her? Or was she just a curiosity to him? A woman who could get along on her own in the mountains. Who knew how to chop wood, build a fire and shoot a gun.

Her mutt had dragged a wet, muddy stick down to the dock. She got it away from him and flung it into the lake. "Fetch, Jake," she urged. "Come on, fetch."

He didn't move.

"You slug, Jake."

"I'm assuming you're speaking to your dog," Jake Farr said, joining her on the dock. "But if you ask me, I wouldn't jump in that cold water to go after a stupid stick, either."

Again Patience felt a surge of warmth at seeing him. It was getting worse, not better, each time he came close to her. And he was close. If she tried to put a few more inches between them she'd land up in the icy lake herself.

"Swimming's good exercise," she said.

"No doubt. When do you take your first dip?"

"Memorial Day, just to say I've done it. I last about ten seconds. I'm not into frostbite swimming."

"When does the water get warm?"

"It doesn't. It gets comfortable, though, around mid-July."

He nodded, acknowledging her words. He seemed content as he looked out across the quiet lake. "Do you go canoeing?"

"Every chance I get. Jake and I go together."

His smile settled on her. "Sounds fun. Think it'll be warm enough to get out on the water today?"

Before she could think—before she could come to her senses—she nodded and said sure. In another minute, she and Jake Farr were heading up to her shed to get out her canoe and paddles and make sure they were lakeworthy.

If she'd been aware of him in her cabin, out on the dock, what would happen when she got into a canoe with him? Then for sure she'd have no place to run. She'd just have to sit there and paddle along and . . .

"Can you steer a canoe?" she asked.

"Uh-huh."

Good, she thought. At least then she'd have her back to him.

It was a mistake.

Jake steered fine. It wasn't that. And she didn't have to worry about being distracted by having to look at his strong back and dark hair. No, not at all. Instead she was distracted with imagining what *he* was thinking in the stern of the canoe looking at *her*.

In the middle of the quiet, still lake, with a clear, sunny sky overhead and the mountains all around them, she could feel Jake Farr's eyes on her. It was all she could do not to swing around suddenly and catch him at it. But she didn't want to capsize the canoe.

Jake was on the end of the dock, barking at them. His human counterpart had refused to take him along on his first outing on the unfamiliar lake. Patience had concurred. Her dog had not, however, and made his displeasure known.

"Does anyone in the Madrid household suffer in silence?" Jake asked.

"People say you always know where you stand with a Madrid."

"I can see why."

Her voice was a little hoarse and that tingling of pure sexual awareness was back, throwing off her paddling rhythm. She wondered if she was just imagining things. Maybe Jake Farr wasn't looking at her in that way at all. Maybe all she was to him was Terrence Terwilliger's nutty sister-in-law.

Then again, maybe not.

She wondered how long he planned to stick around. And what she'd do with herself when he was gone.

The wind picked up, rocking the canoe and penetrating Patience's sweater. She'd skipped her Windbreaker. For March it was a warm wind—which meant it didn't freeze her skin on contact—and she didn't mind it. Also, given the male presence behind her, she welcomed the cool air on her overheated body. Between the exercise of paddling the canoe and the effort to control her vigorous imagination, she was close to melting.

"Shall we head closer to shore?" Jake suggested.

"Sounds good."

With strong, rhythmic strokes, he steered the canoe across the lake. Patience hardly had to paddle at all. It was a nice change from her outings with her lazy dog, who continuously had to be reminded to keep still and not jump out. She pointed out the other cabins on the lake.

"Yes," Jake said dryly, "I saw them last night."

"Oh, that's right. Tilly sent you the long way round, you know."

"What do you mean?"

"It's easier to go up one more exit on the interstate—it's not so remote—and to take the second left off the main road instead of the first. You'd have come to my cabin from the north—it's only about a half mile. Tilly obviously wanted you to think I lived further out in the sticks than I really do."

"Why?"

"How do I know?"

She was more frustrated with her sister than irritated. What was she supposed to do about Tilly? Wait until she returned to New York and wring her neck? Worry?

"You're worried about your sister, aren't you?" Jake asked.

Patience sighed. "I don't know. She's so wrong about me that maybe I'm wrong about her, too. But no matter what, she's acting weird. I..." She clammed up. She'd almost confided in Jake her sister's comments about her marriage. Feeling his eyes boring through her layers of clothes didn't mean she should forget family loyalty. "I don't know what to do, frankly."

"Let's head back to the cabin," Jake said in a quiet, undemanding way. "We can talk there."

She shuddered with a sudden, strange and wholly inappropriate sense of loneliness and longing. To have someone to talk to. To share her troubles and concerns with. To laugh with. Six months ago, she'd have snorted at such sentimentality. She'd relished her winter alone in the cabin with her computer and her work. She had friends. Her parents. Tilly. The Madrid cousins. It wasn't as if she didn't have anyone.

But she didn't have a man in her life.

And men were different.

Paddling slowly, they stayed close to shore. Patience could see the signs of spring in the melted snow, the green shoots poking up out of the mud and dead, wet leaves, the tight red buds on the trees. Before too long the weekend and summer people would be making their way north, telling themselves that someday they would live in the Adirondacks year-round when really they wouldn't. It was just as well. The land was fragile. Patience sometimes thought of herself as an intruder in a wilderness so many, including herself, worked to preserve. She tried never to indulge in the arrogance that she wasn't a part of the problem. But how could she stand to give up this life and live in the city year-round?

In an apartment like Jake Farr's...*with* Jake Farr...

She dropped her paddle in the lake, swearing under her breath.

Jake scooped it up as it floated by his end of the canoe and handed it to her. She had to twist around to
take it from him, and nearly dropped it all over again.
Never had she met a man who was even more drop-
dead sexy in real life than in her imagination. Seeing
him was far more unsettling than simply thinking
about him.

His expression was something between knowing
and amused. "Distracted?"

She smiled feebly. "It's been one of those days."

And it wasn't even noon, she thought. Her hands
were shaking. In the bright sunlight, his eyes seemed
even darker, and she noticed the muscles in his arms
and shoulders, the flatness of his abdomen, the close
fit of his jeans on his thighs. He didn't look at all like
what she thought a New York businessman ought to
look like.

Facing front, she paddled furiously, but her rhythm
was off and she wished she'd steered after all. Finally
Jake quietly suggested she just let him get them ashore.
Annoyed with herself, she set her dripping paddle in
the canoe and placed her hands on her lap. She was
unaccustomed to letting anyone have so much control over her, even if it was just a few yards to the dock.

The hound was barking up a storm.

"Oh, you're just jealous," she called to him.

Jake steered the canoe parallel to the dock, holding
on to the post. "Why don't you get out here and I'll
pull up on shore?"

She said sure. She'd had about enough of canoeing with Jake Farr, anyway. It wasn't him. He wasn't doing anything except being himself. It was her. Her reaction to him. Her disturbing questions about her own life, her own choices. Whether he'd meant to or not, the man had thrown a big fat monkey wrench into her world.

Of course, it wasn't *his* intentions that had landed them on Central Park West and now in the Adirondacks together. It was Tilly's. *She'd* thrown a monkey wrench into her sister's world.

Patience needed a warm fire, hot tea and a cold shower.

And her cabin to herself.

Grabbing hold of the post, she hoisted herself up onto the dock. Her feet were still in the canoe when her idiotic dog pushed past her, throwing her off balance. Then he jumped over her, and she realized he was heading for the canoe.

"Jake," Patience yelled, "you idiot!"

Naturally Jake Farr thought she was talking to him. "What?" he asked, confused, until his canine friend leaped into—or partly into—the canoe. "Good God, you won't fit, you nut."

But it was too late.

The canoe tipped. First the dog went. Then Jake Farr yelled something very pointed and non-urbane as he went head-over-heels into the water. Patience, half horrified, half hysterical with laughter, was left hanging on to the dock. Her feet splashed into the water up to her knees, but damned if she'd let go and submerge herself in the icy lake. The dog immediately beelined for shore, looking confused and a little insulted. He wouldn't have any idea that he'd caused his own dunking.

She'd lost Jake Farr.

Then there was a splash behind her, and a colorful description of just what body parts were about to freeze and fall off into "this godforsaken lake."

Patience tried not to laugh. She didn't try too hard because she was more concerned with keeping her own precious body parts out of the frigid water. But she did try. Hooking one leg up onto the dock, she glanced back, just in time to see Jake Farr tearing for shore in the thigh-deep water. He was drenched head to toe and cursing soundly. The other Jake was barking furiously at him. When Jake got to shore, the dog decided to shake off, soaking him further. Jake threatened to cook him over a spit for dinner.

It was more than Patience could stand. She positively howled with laughter at the sight of Jake Putnam Farr of New York City soaked to the bone, having it out with a waterlogged dog. She would have doubled over if she hadn't been trying to keep herself from getting just as wet.

The two Jakes heard her laughing. The human one was clearly not amused.

"That's it," he said, and bounded toward her.

Patience struggled to get herself up onto the dock, but she was weak with laughter, barely able to hold on, and now she had the added pressure of Jake Farr coming after her.

He planted his squishy sneakers right at the post to which she was so desperately clinging and squatted down on one knee. He was breathing hard and there were droplets of water clinging to his face. If possible, he was even sexier dripping Adirondack lake water. Breathtaking, really.

"Having a little trouble?" His tone was downright menacing.

"I'd rather not get any wetter than I already am...."

"Oh, I'm sure."

He made no move to help her.

She noticed his dark, wet hair and the way his shirt clung to his chest and arms. "If you'd move," she said, "I could give a good heave and get out of this position."

"Is that right?"

"Jake, it wasn't my fault—"

"You laughed," he pointed out.

"It was *funny.*"

"Do you know how cold that water is?"

"Yes. My left foot is still in it."

"But not your whole body."

She was doomed. The man was definitely an eye-for-an-eye type. She ought to just give up and drop in the water, get it over with. But she wasn't the type to surrender without a fight.

"I'm innocent," she said.

He grunted in disbelief. "Sweetheart," he said in a low, seductive voice that further loosened her grip, "you're a lot of things, but innocent isn't one of them."

Then he grabbed her arm, held her suspended, neither pulling her up onto the dock nor pushing her all the way into the lake.

"Debating whether to toss me in headfirst or feetfirst?"

"Neither."

He took her other arm and hoisted her up as if she was no heavier than a sack of onions and held her close against his cold, wet chest.

"I was just debating," he said, "whether we should warm up by the fire."

"Or?"

He gave her a slow, piratical smile. "Or not."

8

IF IT HAD BEEN any warmer out, Patience was convinced they'd have made love right out there on the dock. As it was, Jake had no choice but to release her, and she dashed up to the cabin ahead of him, half-frozen by the time she got there. She consoled herself that Jake Farr was even colder than she was. She quickly shoved two logs on the fire and peeled off her icy socks, hanging them on a pot-warmer above the wood stove. A sense of responsibility—that, at the moment, had nothing to do with affection—compelled her to towel off her dog, who dove under the stove at first opportunity. Apollo and Aphrodite had already vacated the front room for her bedroom and were probably happy to have avoided the commotion.

Jake Farr could have passed for a big, cold, wet dog himself with all his growling.

"Better get those wet things off," Patience told him unnecessarily. "Wouldn't want you to get hypothermia."

He glared at her, tearing off his layers of upscale mountain clothes. Patience tried not to stare. It was difficult. He had truly impressive shoulders and his abdomen was flat and obviously hard.

He threw down his heavy, soaked sweater and unfastened the top button of his pants.

Patience turned away abruptly. She wasn't used to having a half-frozen man undressing in her cabin.

Jake laughed. His laugh was soft, amused, sexy. An invitation.

"I can go into the bathroom," he said.

"It's colder in there. I—I'll duck into my bedroom and get some dry clothes on myself."

He watched her a moment. "Suit yourself."

As she walked past him, she noticed the purple tint to his lips. "You'd better get some warm liquids in you, too."

"You know the best cure for hypothermia, don't you?"

She did, but chose not to say so.

"Another person's warm body," he answered for her.

"Well, I'm not that warm myself."

That laugh again. A touch of incredulity had crept in. "Oh, I don't know about that."

She dashed into her bedroom and shut her door quickly and firmly behind her. She *was* warm, all right. Burning up. Never mind that her feet ached as they began to thaw. The rest of her—the crucial parts—might just have come out of the wood stove they were so hot.

"Tilly," she breathed, "what have you done to me?"

Her life had been so ordered. So sensible. A little eccentric by other people's accounts, perhaps, but she'd been free. No more. Jake Farr had turned her peaceful existence on its head and given it a ferocious shake.

It wasn't his fault. He hadn't meant to do anything of the sort. He was Tilly's victim, as well. Probably out in the front room cursing his fate. Wondering how the hell he'd ended up flipped out of a canoe by a dog into a cold Adirondack lake. Thinking he couldn't get back to New York fast enough.

Then again, who knew what a good head-to-toe dunking in forty-degree water did to a man?

You know the best cure for hypothermia, don't you?

Probably didn't matter who she was. Not right now when he was cold and she was the only woman around. Maybe she wasn't being fair to him, but since when were sex and romance and hormones fair? Because it wasn't just his obvious, if dubious, attraction to her that was troubling her. It was her attraction to him. It went beyond dreams and fantasies. It had begun to involve not who she thought Jake Farr could be, but who he was.

With a groan of pure frustration—physical *and* mental—she changed her clothes top to bottom, putting on her oldest, baggiest jeans, a cheap sweatshirt and Uncle Isaiah's ancient red chamois shirt. She braided her hair. Any number of curly strands wouldn't stay in the braid, but she ignored them, letting them poke out and fall where they would. If nothing else, she'd obliterate any lingering image Jake Farr had of her at dinner in New York—elegant, feminine, sophisticated. She peeked in the mirror. This was who she was—sloppy, casual, down-to-earth.

"Are you dressed?" she called out to the front room.

"More or less. You can come out now."

What did "more or less" mean? Feeling more nervous than the time she'd had to roust a potentially rabid fox off her porch, Patience ventured into the front room. Her knees were weak, and not from her morning adventures. She balled her hands up inside Uncle Isaiah's soft, tattered sleeves, which were several inches too long even for her. The heat from the stove immediately warmed her body.

And so did the sight of Jake Farr.

He'd pulled a chair from the table up close to the fire and sat with his legs stretched out. His bare feet were tucked up under her dog, who'd collapsed in total exhaustion from his role in their ordeal. He had on a black chamois shirt which he'd left unbuttoned, nothing but dark chest hairs and taut abdomen underneath. He'd put on black sweatpants. She had a sudden impulse to run her hand over his thigh to feel the juxtaposition of the soft, fleecy fabric over his hard muscles.

"I had visions of a mountain run," he told her, explaining his sweatpants.

"I'm sorry things aren't working out the way you'd planned."

"I don't know if I had any plans. Hopes, perhaps. Expectations, dreads. But not plans. Your sister had me thinking I might have to cart you off to the loony bin." He studied her a moment. "You okay?"

She nodded, feigning—probably badly—calm. "Fine."

Before she could see in his eyes whether or not he knew she was lying, she walked around his chair and checked the fire in the wood stove. It was cooking right along, but she added another log, anyway, just to have something to do. Her only hope was to keep busy.

"Still cold?" he asked from behind her.

"A little."

"Sit by the fire, then. There's room."

She looked around at him. "No, there isn't. But it's okay."

"Sure there is," he said in a low, husky voice.

Without another word, he swung one arm around her waist and pulled her down onto his lap. She'd never sat on a man's lap before. Never. It wasn't something she did—hadn't done even in her youth. She landed awkwardly, her heart thudding, and automatically balanced herself by placing a hand on his chest. Another mistake. Despite his unexpected dip in the lake, his skin was warm to the touch, and the muscles were as solid as she'd imagined.

"You, um, seem to have warmed up."

"My feet are still ice blocks, but they'll recover."

She sat rock-still. "I'm not a small woman—you must be uncomfortable."

There came that spine-melting laugh again. "You could call it that."

She blushed. She who had grown up among the freewheeling, freethinking, free-speaking Madrids. She who had been on her own for more than a decade and had grown up around animals and men and knew what was what. She was not what anyone would call an ignorant innocent. She wasn't unworldly.

But she wasn't stupid, either.

She knew she was blushing not because of what Jake had said but because she'd thought it even before he'd said it. She'd noticed what the rugby-weight fabric of his sweatpants did nothing to hide. He was aroused.

"You're not an easy woman to figure out, Patience Madrid," he said quietly.

"I'm just . . ." She paused and licked her lips, aware that he was watching her. "I'm just trying to be myself."

"I know." He shifted so that she was thrown up closer to his chest; his arms were wrapped around her waist. She felt warm, feminine even, in Uncle Isaiah's old shirt. "That's what's so intriguing."

They were eye to eye, the man from New York and the woman from the mountains, and all Patience could think was how much she wanted to kiss him, wanted him to kiss her. She could almost feel it happening. She could taste the moistness of his mouth. Feel his warm tongue circling and melding with hers.

"Jake . . ."

And then it was happening. She couldn't have said who made the first move, didn't care, only closed her eyes and allowed herself to be enveloped by the sensation of the kiss.

His hand curved around her bottom, and the intimacy of his touch electrified her. She relaxed against him, her breasts crushed against his chest, as their kiss became more deep, more abandoned. Its effects spread throughout her whole body. She could feel its effect on him pressing against her thigh.

"Jake . . . I didn't mean for this to happen."

His eyes were so dark, liquid with wanting. "Do you want it to?"

She didn't hesitate. "Yes." He lifted her easily—she might have been an armload of wood—and she laughed. "Does passion give you superhuman strength, Mr. Farr?"

He smiled. "You're fit, Miss Madrid, but you're not even close to being heavy." He drew her up higher in his arms, tight against his chest, so that she could feel his heart beating along with her own. For a second she didn't know where his began and hers ended. "I could carry you all day."

She wasn't sure if it was bravado, kindness or the truth. "Pray you never have to."

Bursting into her bedroom, he carried her to the bed. She still used Uncle Isaiah's old horsehair mattress and cast-iron frame, but she'd added her own touches to her bedroom—a slate-blue handwoven spread, appliquéd pillows, pottery lamps, antique cross-stitched samplers, a collection of scented candles in a wide variety of holders. It was an eclectic room, feminine and cheerful, and she saw Jake looking around in obvious surprise.

"What did you expect?" she asked, amused. "Gun racks and trophies?"

"I had heard stories."

"There's a lot of Uncle Isaiah here still, but a lot of me, too. Things don't have to stay the same. I can accommodate change."

Could you accommodate Jake Farr? Add him to Uncle Isaiah's old cabin?

But she only formed the question, didn't bother with an answer, as Jake laid her on the bed and settled alongside her, their two shapes oddly, perfectly suited. He lifted her arm and started to roll up the frayed, dangling sleeve, then broke off. "Let's just get rid of this thing altogether."

"I know it's not very sexy—"

"On the contrary," he murmured, sliding the old shirt off her shoulders. "It invites one to speculate on the possibilities."

She wasn't entirely sure what he meant, but his voice, his touch, his eyes all combined to make her feel sensual and wanted, connected to him in a way that made her ache with a wild mix of emotions she couldn't pin down or separate. But she didn't care.

"Actually," he went on, "it's your socks. There's something curiously erotic about a woman in her stocking feet."

She smiled. "You're an unusual man, Jake Farr."

"I accept that as a compliment."

But she could see he was distracted, not really paying attention to what he was saying. He dropped Uncle Isaiah's shirt off her side of the bed onto the floor, which entailed rolling half on top of her. He was reasonably warm all over, except for his feet, which might have just come from the icebox. She rubbed her woolen socks over them.

She said, "If you're cold—"

"Getting warmer every second."

Jake held her closely against him. His breath tickled her face and the weight of his broad chest pressed against her breasts. Their hips were locked. He'd hooked one leg over hers, and they were united almost as if they were one body. With his finger, he brushed stray hairs from her forehead, but they flopped back, and he moved on, slowly tracing a path down her hairline to her ear, then across her jaw to her mouth. He outlined her lips. She kissed the tip of his finger and smiled.

"Oh, Patience," he whispered, lowering his mouth to hers.

It was a slow, romantic, generous kiss, giving more than taking, asking more than demanding. Patience drank in its every nuance, trying to discover the man lying next to her through his kiss. He tightened his arms around her, drew her solidly against him. Her shirt had come untucked. He slid his fingers underneath it. She shivered.

"Are my hands cold?" he asked.

"Not cold—just a bit cool. But that's not why I shivered."

He smiled. "I didn't think so."

"Sure of yourself, aren't you?"

Her tone was teasing, but his expression turned serious and he shook his head, gently rubbing his thumbs along her sides. "No, not at all. I'm just sure that this is what I want—that I've been waiting a long, long time for you to come into my life." His eyes seemed to darken as he shifted next to her. She had to roll onto her back to maintain the close view she wanted of him, of his square jaw and strong shoulders. "And when you respond to me...when I feel your need..." He shrugged. "It gives me hope."

Her throat was dry, constricted, but she couldn't figure out why, and when she spoke, her words came out in an unexpected hoarse whisper. "Hope for what?"

"For us."

And his mouth descended to hers once more, as his palms slid up her stomach to her breasts, lifting her shirt. His fingers skimmed her lacy bra. She sensed his surprise. Pulling his mouth from hers, he glanced down. Her bra had a fairly racy cut and was the color of pumpkins.

"I don't think anyone makes woodswoman bras," she said.

"What other surprises do you have in store?"

Matching bikini underpants, something he could discover in due time. "Oh," she said evasively, "you never know."

He'd started to unclasp her bra when their four-legged friend wandered into the bedroom and barked, obviously not sure what was going on. Patience tried to get rid of him. But Jake was a stubborn beast, and New York had spoiled him if not, as she feared, completely ruined him. He leaped onto the bed. He was still damp from his dip in the lake and smelled like wet mittens.

Patience jerked up straight. "*No!* Jake—Jake, off the bed. Now. You know it can't take this much weight."

He stood up on all fours and panted in their faces.

"Good Lord," Jake Farr said, and rolled sideways off the bed.

"*Off, you mutt!*"

She gave him a good shove, and finally he got the hint and, with a dangerous creaking of slats, bounded onto the floor. Patience groaned and fell back onto her pillows. Now she also smelled like wet wool.

Jake—the one she *wanted* on her bed—reached down and tugged her shirt back over her pumpkin bra. "Your dog has a point."

"What? What kind of point? The stupid mutt has no sense of timing—"

"Not intentionally, no." Jake straightened, his eyes not on her now, but focused on the hemlock outside her window. Without looking at her, he said, "The point is, we haven't talked."

"Talked," she repeated.

He nodded.

And, with a long sigh of exasperation, she agreed.

"I'll put the kettle on for tea," he said, and withdrew from her bedroom.

Patience glared at her dog. Unrepentant—indeed, probably unaware he'd done a thing wrong all day— he followed his new friend out to the front room. She heard the clattering of the wood stove, the running of water. Humming. Well, she wondered, when Jake Farr said they needed to talk, did he mean he, she or they should do the talking?

And was he being noble or had her dog's intrusion catapulted him back to his senses, reminding him that he was on a horsehair mattress in the middle of the woods with the younger sister of his best friend's wife?

"Well," she muttered, "everyone says if it's one thing you've got it's guts. So go find out."

After all, she'd never been one to shy from reality.

But she'd never had such a pleasant, tempting fantasy as making love with Jake Putnam Farr. It wouldn't be an easy one to surrender to reality.

"I'M WORRIED ABOUT TILLY," Patience said.

Jake studied her from across the table. He'd made English breakfast tea. For lunch, he'd grilled a couple of cheese sandwiches on the wood stove and opened a can of pineapple. "Why?" he asked.

"She hasn't been herself."

"That's what she says about you."

Patience waved a hand. "Yeah, but she's wrong about me. Saying I'm depressed—well, if it wasn't some harebrained scheme to get us together—"

"Considering what we were just about to do," Jake interrupted quietly, "I'm not sure 'harebrained' is the word I'd choose."

"Harebrained in the sense it was too obvious, too unlikely to work. Not that it didn't work..." She groaned. "Oh, never mind. The point is, I'm *not* depressed. I think Tilly's projecting her own depression onto me. You know, misery loves company."

Jake bit into the second half of his sandwich, which oozed melted cheese. He seemed content with their simple lunch. He said, "I don't see Matilda as being depressed."

"Troubled, then."

He said nothing.

Patience sighed, wishing she hadn't started on this subject. Divulging family problems just wasn't the Madrid style. But Jake had begun to feel like family....

"I think she and Terrence are having marital problems."

"What makes you think that?"

"Tilly said so."

"I see."

Patience used her fork to lift a slice of pineapple out of the can and set it on the edge of her plate. Inelegant, but functional. "She told me they were going on separate vacations to work on certain issues in their marriage—she to Arizona, Terrence to Florida. But now I know there's more to it than she's telling me." Patience went on to explain the lie about the Hidden Camel and Hidden Flamingo resorts.

"Why do you think she made them up?" he asked.

"She wouldn't level with me when we talked. I think it's just a symptom of her confused state of mind, her lack of trust. I don't know. If I knew, maybe I wouldn't be so worried." She exhaled, suddenly no longer hungry. "But I don't know."

"So you are worried."

"I can't help it."

"You and your sister are close?"

She nodded. "Always have been."

"That's nice. My brother and sister and I . . . well, we have our moments. But since I'm not married and producing children, don't live in the suburbs, don't work nine to five—we don't have as much in common as we once did. Sometimes it gets in the way of our relationship. Sometimes it enhances our relationship. It just depends."

Patience narrowed her eyes at him, thinking. "Are you suggesting that because my life and Tilly's are so different we're no longer communicating? That we have nothing in common?"

"I'm saying," he paused, pushing back his chair, "that you and your sister maybe don't have as much in common as you once did. Your lives are different. That could skew the way you see each other."

"It could."

"You sound dubious."

"That's because I *am* dubious. Jake, you have to understand the Madrid family. We never were like other people. We had Uncle Isaiah, the hermit, and eccentric archaeologist parents who really weren't like other parents at all. I mean, we never went to amusement parks. We went on treks in the woods to hunt for arrowheads. We didn't even have a television set—I still don't. I could always count on Tilly to understand me, and she could count on me to understand her. We weren't like normal suburban families."

"Just what *is* a normal suburban family? I'm not sure there is such a thing. All families are by definition unique in some way." He grabbed the pineapple can and lifted out a couple slices. "But I'm not denying the uniqueness or the peculiarities of your upbringing. I'm just suggesting that perhaps you and your sister's lives have taken such different paths that you can't count on each other always to understand. Maybe this time you don't. And she doesn't."

Patience was still reluctant to see his point, despite the voice inside her that said it was a valid one. "What's there not to understand? I'm not depressed. She said so herself. And she's the one who told me her marriage was on the skids."

"Her words?"

"Well, she doesn't say things like 'on the skids' anymore. I don't remember her exact words."

"Isn't it a possibility," he said carefully, "that you and your sister are both jumping to erroneous conclusions about each other?"

"*I* didn't lie about where I was staying."

He sighed. "That is a bit odd, I agree, but perhaps there's an innocent explanation."

"Such as?"

He thought a moment, then shook his head. "Can't think of one."

"I wish I knew where they really were staying, together *or* separately. I don't think I can stand another week of not knowing. Next she'll call you and tell you I—who knows what? Depressed is bad enough."

"That you've taken up wearing sexy pumpkin underclothes?"

"Jake Farr, if you tell her that—"

He laughed. "It's our secret, I promise."

Their secret. It sounded delicious. And scary.

But Jake had grown thoughtful again. "I don't know if I should suggest this . . ."

At his hesitation, Patience, her curiosity piqued, prodded him. "Suggest what?"

He looked at her. "There's a chance I can find out where they're staying."

"How?"

"Terrence and I use the same travel agent who's a mutual friend. It's not a guarantee, but I could ask."

"Could," Patience observed, "but does that mean you will?"

"If we *are* the victims of an elaborate scheme by either Terrence or Matilda, I think we owe it to ourselves to find out sooner rather than later, don't you?"

"What do you mean?"

"I mean," he said, leaning over the table, his dark eyes commanding her undivided attention, "that your concern for your sister and her role in our coming together is a distraction. For both of us. I want to get to the bottom of it before—" He shook his head, not finishing. "Let's just leave it at that."

It wasn't easy, but she did. She thought of how close they'd come to making love on her horsehair mattress in the next room. Of how close—how damned close—she was to falling in love with this man. Where would they be in another week when Tilly came home?

"This travel agent's in New York?"

"Yes."

"Can you call?"

He shook his head, rising. "I think this is something I should handle face to face. If I get moving, I can reach her before she leaves the office."

Patience couldn't understand her sudden disappointment—she felt devastated that he was leaving. Her cabin was her home. Her space. And she wanted him in it.

It just didn't make sense.

"You'll call me when you get an answer?"

"Call you?" He frowned at her. "I was assuming you and your entourage would be coming with me. We can take your car since I assume it's set up for animals."

From his enthusiasm, Patience guessed he hadn't really noticed her Jeep in the driveway. She'd noticed his Acura. Her dog would have loved to ride in the passenger seat. But she supposed that with a little imagination she and the two Jakes and the two cats could all fit in her Jeep, although it would be a struggle. Regardless of how they traveled, she couldn't believe how excited she was at the prospect of heading back to the Big Apple.

She tossed her sandwich crust under the stove for Jake. "Did you hear that, you hairy beast? It's off to the big city again."

"Yes," Jake Farr said, "and let's not forget a leash, shall we?"

THERE WERE THINGS in his life Jake Farr wished he could go back and undo. The time in college he'd gone to a football game instead of studying for his economics exam. The relationship he'd maintained for far too long in his early twenties with a woman who hated mountain-climbing, hated Wall Street, and really, she finally admitted, hated him. The ten thousand dollars he'd thrown down the tubes on a friend's nutso idea for a doomed company. Stupid bets on hockey games. Bad decisions.

They paled in comparison to having told Patience Madrid they could all go to New York in her Jeep. Definitely something he'd undo if he had the chance.

He should have inspected her Jeep before making such a daring suggestion. He should have asked to sample her driving style. Taken a cruise around the lake with her at the wheel. Experienced how a mountain woman drove before ending up on the interstate with her.

He should have considered her hairy, muddy dog and her temporary custody of her sister's two New York cats. Asked himself where he thought the animals were supposed to sit.

Where the hell had his head been?

He knew. His head—his entire body—was still feeling the effects of having come so close to making love to this wild, teal-eyed redhead.

It wasn't that she was a bad driver. She stayed between the lines on the interstate and only exceeded the speed limit when she passed, if simply because her rusting hulk of a Jeep couldn't be trusted to maintain a high rate of speed. But she didn't sit still behind the wheel. At unpredictable moments she'd pluck a cat off her lap or reach back and scrounge around for a dropped dog bone or stick an arm in front of Jake for a tattered map in the overflowing glove compartment. It was nerve-racking.

"If you'll just tell me," he would say, "I can do things for you."

"Oh. Right. I'm not used to having a passenger."

Patience Madrid, he decided, was used to doing everything on her own. He wondered if she could change, if she *wanted* to change. Not give up her independence, but merely share it with another person. Him, for instance.

He shifted uncomfortably at the thought. Maybe he was allergic to cats and his mind wasn't working properly. Aphrodite was curled up on his lap, purring. Apollo had perched himself on the headrest of his seat; a sudden braking and Jake would have the beast clinging—claws out, no doubt—to the back of his neck. Jake the dog had the back seat to himself. Even so, he would give his human counterpart sullen, jealous looks for confiscating the passenger seat.

Never was Jake so delighted to see the New York skyline.

Patience's Jeep being what it was, he felt every pothole, every bump, grate, crack in the road. And in New York there were many. He didn't care. He was home. She stopped in front of the Terwilligers' building on Central Park West, and Jake offered to park her Jeep while she tended her animals.

"Hope it goes better than last time," she said, grinning.

He remembered—he would never forget—Saturday morning, the elevator doors parting, and the big, hairy, ugly, slobbering dog leaping inside with him. He'd thought he was a dead man. And he'd seen Patience Madrid for the first time as he was pinned to the elevator wall. Had it been fate?

More likely, the hand of Matilda Terwilliger.

Cats, dog and redhead disembarked from the Jeep. Jake thought he saw the doorman blanch.

Parking the Jeep was an adventure. It handled better than he expected, but for the first time in all his years in New York, pedestrians actually got out of the way when they saw him coming. The skinny parking attendant recognized the all-too-memorable vehicle.

"What happened to the lady and the dog?"

Jake battled an inclination to disavow any knowledge of Patience Madrid and her dog. But he said, "They're back at her sister's apartment."

"So she really is Mrs. Terwilliger's sister?"

"She is."

The attendant shook his head, the New Yorker who'd now seen everything. "Well, I guess you never know."

"I guess you don't."

At the Terwilligers' building, one of the doormen asked him how long he and Miss Madrid would be staying. Jake noticed white cat hair on the man's uniform and assumed Patience's entrance had not been uneventful. "Her dog..." the doorman said, but shook his head, not going on.

Jake found Patience in the cavernous master bathroom attempting to bathe Apollo and Aphrodite. Two monogrammed pure white Egyptian cotton towels, undoubtedly never intended for cat use, were set out on the counter.

"You made it up here all right?" he asked.

"Oh, sure. Aphrodite tried to claw my ear off and Jake got loose, but the doorman grabbed him and offered to take Aphrodite for me. Nice, huh?"

Jake doubted the doorman had tried to be nice. More likely he'd tried to avoid having the entire lobby destroyed by the three animals.

"Now, Apollo," Patience said, plopping an unhappy cat onto one of the towels, which she proceeded to unfold around him. "You'll live. That wasn't even a real bath."

From the look of him, Apollo didn't agree. He quickly made his escape past Jake. Before Aphrodite could follow him through the door, Patience snatched her up, plopped her in the tub and unceremoniously removed any traces of her Adirondack sojourn from her beautiful fur.

It occurred to Jake he could stand there and watch Patience Madrid the rest of the day. But he said, "I'm off to see what I can find out about Terrence and your sister's whereabouts. You'll be okay here?"

Aphrodite twisted free and raced out of the bathroom, dripping suds and water. Patience laughed, though Jake could see scratches on her forearms. "If I don't have a rebellion on my hands. See you soon?"

He sensed an awkwardness, a reserve, she hadn't exhibited on her turf up north or even sitting so close to him on the trip south. Perhaps it was just being alone with him in the huge bathroom, a tub plenty big enough for two right behind her. His mouth went dry as he considered the possibilities.

"I'll be back a.s.a.p.," he said and dashed out of the bathroom before he could stop himself from exploring those possibilities.

First things first, he told himself. If he was ever to have Patience's full attention, he first had to track down her sister and brother-in-law. After that . . .

Well, who knew?

One thing was certain: his apartment renovations would include a tub just as big as the one on Central Park West.

"YOU'RE SURE?" Jake asked his friend an hour later.

Emmie Dalton sighed, exercising more patience with him than he probably deserved, considering what he'd just talked her into doing. "Of course I'm sure. I made the reservations myself. Just how sick is Matilda's sister?"

Jake bit his lower lip. He'd hated lying. "Emmie—"

She narrowed her eyes at him. She was slim and petite, with neat black hair and a deceptively cute smile. Her black designer suit gave a more accurate impression of the imposing, successful and smart woman that she was. She'd become a top Madison Avenue travel agent through her own guts and hard work. Jake had been friends with her for years.

She sighed, watching him with knowing eyes. "Jake Putnam, you lied to me."

He nodded.

"Rat."

"I'm sorry."

"Did you have a good reason?"

"I think so."

"The Terwilligers are good clients. *And* they're friends." She leaned back in her ergonomically correct chair, rattling a cheap ballpoint between two fingers. "If I didn't rat them out over sickness and death, it'd better be over love and romance. I like a happy ending."

He cleared his throat. "I'll explain when this thing's resolved."

She wasn't going to let him off that easily. "Does this 'thing' involve the sister?"

Jake pretended not to hear her. "Thanks, Emmie." He was on his feet. "I promise I'll keep your name out of it."

"She's always sounded like your type to me. Mountain woman—skins animals herself, from what I hear."

The Patience Madrid myth. Jake had seen no evidence of hunting or trapping in her cabin. He'd even checked her freezer—what meat was there had come from the grocery store.

"I'll talk to you soon," he said.

"Jake Farr, are you in love?"

She was grinning. His own friends wouldn't sympathize with his dilemma. They'd be amused, entertained because he'd fallen head over heels for—

Just who the devil *was* Patience Madrid?

"Well," Emmie said, "if you ask me, it's about time."

Since she'd just done him a remarkable favor, Jake didn't point out that he hadn't asked.

She continued. "You end up on New York's list of most eligible bachelors one more time and we women are going to start a hall of fame for all you incorrigible bastards who're determined to remain unattached. Disqualify you from getting on the list. 'Eligible' implies a certain willingness to engage in a long-term relationship."

This from a woman who regularly stated her own determination to avoid marriage. "Look who's talking . . ."

"Don't start on my love life when I'm lecturing you on yours. Besides, I've got real work to do around here." She reached for her telephone and waved a hand at him in dismissal. "Go."

Jake went, glad for his friends in New York, his life here. Could he give them all up for an isolated mountain cabin?

On his way back to Central Park West, he stopped in at his office. All was well there. Naturally. He returned a few calls and headed back to the apartment.

Patience was in the kitchen, unloading a monstrous bag from Zabar's that included, she informed him, a sample of ten different dishes she couldn't resist and six kinds of dessert.

"Any luck?" she asked.

"If you mean did I find out where they're staying, yes, I did."

"And?"

Taking her by the wrist, he led her into the living room with its magnificent view of Central Park. He pointed south. "There."

"What do mean? Florida, the moon, where?"

"The Plaza."

"What plaza?"

"The Plaza Hotel, Patience."

"You mean the *New York* Plaza?"

He nodded. He could tell she was shocked. He had been, too. And angry. Instantly angry. Patience Madrid wasn't one to ponder how she felt. Jake himself was still deciding whether or not he wanted to strangle the Terwilligers or fall down laughing.

Or whether he should worry. This kind of subterfuge wasn't like Terrence. *Was* his marriage on the rocks?

"We should discuss this," he said.

She shot him a look, in no mood to discuss anything. "What's there to discuss? My sister lied to me. She's made me the victim of some elaborate scam. She—she's acting weird."

But, Jake noticed, Patience didn't seem particularly surprised that her sister had never left New York, nor particularly insulted, and not the least bit hurt. She was just angry. Jake couldn't tell how angry. He judiciously kept silent, following her as she stamped into the guest room she'd appropriated from him.

"What're you doing?" he asked.

"Packing."

"Patience . . ." He sighed, watching her stuff things back into a large canvas tote bag. "Look, you don't have to leave. Let's have dinner and talk this over. It's a long drive back to the mountains."

She angled her hot teal eyes at him. "Who said I was heading home? *That* would be surrendering."

Pulling her bag off the bed, she carried it past him, out into the hall, where she dropped it on the polished wood floor and shoved it against the wall. She was breathing hard. Her cheeks were peachy red. She'd changed out of her driving clothes into rust-colored leggings and a big chenille sweater in a slightly lighter shade of rust.

"Then where are you going?" Jake asked calmly.

Her eyes met his. They were glittering, fiery. She caught her breath and seemed to relax, if only a little. And instead of out-and-out anger in her expression, he saw her zest for adventure, her determination, the years of affection and trust between two sisters that virtually nothing would shatter.

But she smiled, a small, self-deprecating smile. "I'm going to check into the Plaza Hotel."

He'd been afraid of something like that. "Patience—"

But he stopped himself. He remembered something Terrence had said not long after he and Matilda had married. *"There's one thing I've learned, Jake— it's never to come between my wife and her sister. There's a bond between them that you rarely get to see between two people. They're different as night and day, but I've never seen two sisters more devoted to each other, who know each other better. It's really something."*

Indeed it was.

"If my sister's in trouble," Patience said, "I need to know."

"What if she's not?"

Her jaw tightened. "Then I need to know that, too."

"For what purpose?"

She headed back toward the kitchen. Without turning, she said, "So I can figure out whether her death ought to be slow or quick!"

Bravado, Jake decided. "I think you're like your dog," he called to her. "All bark and no bite."

Dead silence. Not even a peep from the kitchen.

A woman to be reckoned with, Patience Madrid. Whistling to show just how unconcerned he was at the host of possible reactions she might have at his comment, he sauntered down the hall.

Diving headfirst from the kitchen doorway, she blindsided him with a massive tackle, pushing him against the wall. She was strong. And fit. Willing to take risks. And she had the element of surprise in her favor. But in her actions Jake clearly saw a woman who still thought of him as Terrence Terwilliger's best friend, a New Yorker, which, in her estimation, wasn't up to a good fight with a woman who knew how to fell trees and build fires.

"All right, Jake Farr, I'll show you bark and bite." But she'd underestimated him. Jake knew it.

"Mmm," he said, "I wish you would."

She glanced up at him, and in her eyes he saw that she knew she'd made a mistake.

"Don't you dare," she said.

He laughed. "Too late."

With more ease than doubtlessly she'd have liked, he caught her around the torso in an old wrestler's hold, about-faced her and propelled her across the hall, where he pinned her up against the opposite wall.

It took some effort, but he'd thought before he'd acted. He'd known he'd succeed.

"I should have kicked you when I had the chance," Patience told him matter-of-factly. "Never let up on an opponent, right?"

"Right," he said. "You should never have pegged me for a weakling."

"Now, Jake, I never—*No! Don't you dare! No tickling!*"

But her sweater had gotten scrunched up under her breasts, exposing a tempting expanse of bare midriff, and how could he have resisted? She was laughing, pummeling him with her elbows, until finally, with a massive burst of energy and willpower, she spun around against his chest and had at him, seeming instinctively to know all his ticklish spots. They fell to the floor together, legs intertwined, neither willing to give up.

He could have made love to her then and there.

But he didn't. It wasn't willpower or nobility or common sense or even hunger.

It was, he thought, because he cared so damned much about her. She had to put her mind at ease about her sister. Then . . .

Distracted, he'd let her manage to flip him over on his back and climb onto his stomach, straddling him. Her hair had come out of its pins and braid, thick, curly strands of it dangling in her face. She was panting for air. From his vantage point on the floor, he could see her breasts heaving with each gulp of air.

First, her sister.

Then there'd be no stopping him.

PATIENCE LEFT shortly after dinner, looking urban and perfectly capable of getting along on her own in the big city. Jake walked with her out to her cab. He'd offered to carry her bag, but she'd declined. He wondered how many Plaza guests arrived with such unprepossessing luggage.

He noticed the monogram for the first time. "MMT?"

"Matilda Madrid Terwilliger." Patience grinned around at him and she pulled open the cab door. "Her mother-in-law and sister-in-law both gave her monogrammed canvas bags. Do you believe it?"

Knowing the Terwilligers as he did, Jake believed it.

"'Course," Patience said, "Tilly just uses hers for the beach and picnics. I use mine for whatever."

Apparently a night at one of New York City's priciest hotels constituted "whatever."

Which reminded him. "You had no trouble getting a reservation?"

"Huh?"

"A reservation, Patience."

"Hell, it's a big hotel, there won't be a problem." He sighed.

Shoving her tote bag onto the cab seat, she turned to him and frowned. "Jake Farr, I'm not some kind of a rube. I know the Plaza's not your average roadside

motel. I didn't call ahead for a reservation because . . ." Her frown intensified to a glare. "Because
I was *distracted*, okay? But don't you worry, I'll manage just fine."

Since there was no delicate way to ask his next
question, he didn't bother trying to be discreet.
"You're all right for money?"

"I should be. I brought a ton of cash."

He didn't say a word, just imagined her whisking
out a pile of crumpled bills and plopping her monogrammed canvas tote bag on the reservation desk at
the Plaza Hotel. At least she'd decided to leave her dog
with him. But her chances were still less than even that
she'd land a room, even if there was one available. He
wondered what she meant by "a ton of cash," but
didn't ask. As she'd said, she wasn't a rube. She was
a talented, intelligent writer specializing in environmental topics. She'd just penned her first book. She
knew how to book a room in a hotel.

But she was worried about her sister, confused by
her feelings for him, and this was New York. It wasn't
like other places.

She climbed into the cab, and Jake shut the door
behind her, wishing her well. She grinned and waved.

An intrepid woman.

He went back up to the Terwilligers' apartment and,
kicking all animals out of the den and shutting himself in, called Emmie Dalton at home.

"I need a big favor," he told her.

"Two in one day? Gosh, the gossip columnists get hold of this—"

"Emmie, please, this is painful enough as it is."

"Ah, male pride. Well, my friend, don't you worry, one of these days you will, I assure you, be called upon to return these favors. What can I do for you?"

"A room at the Plaza."

"For when?"

"Now. Tonight."

"Well, hell, Jake, you don't ask for much. While I'm at it, you want a five-room suite, champagne, chocolates, a masseuse?"

"Just a room, Emmie," he said patiently. "Can you do it?"

"Of course I can do it," she hissed, insulted. "But you owe me, Jake Putnam Farr."

"I'll remember."

"Damned right you'll remember."

He gave her the details she needed and five minutes later she rang him back. "Done," she said, and hung up.

Mission accomplished, Jake resisted the temptation to build a fire, find a good book and spend the rest of the evening alone in the den. Instead he returned to the outer rooms and dutifully took Patience Madrid's ugly dog for a walk. He was definitely not a New York dog. No one stopped to pet him, no one called him a handsome beast. Mostly people gave them wide berth, if only because Jake looked as if he'd break free of his leash at any moment and turn the city upside down. He wasn't used to the pace of the city, the rules, the tricks of getting along and enjoying life there. Like his mistress, he was used to the freedom of the mountains.

After ten blocks, Jake suspected his canine counterpart would never really feel at home in the city. He'd never belong.

He patted the tired old dog on the head. "What about Patience huh, boy? Think she could ever feel at home here?"

But the dog had no answers, and neither did Jake. So finally, at a slow pace, they headed back to Central Park West.

"YES, MISS MADRID," the formal man behind the Plaza reception desk said, "I have your reservation right here."

"But I don't have a reservation."

He smiled and leaned over, saying in a quiet, conspiratorial voice, "Emmie Dalton said you might be surprised. I spoke to her myself a few minutes ago. She's taken care of everything."

Patience's bag bounced against her knee. "Everything?"

"Your entire tab is taken care of, including any room service you might wish to order."

Who the hell was Emmie Dalton?

Patience looked around the elegant lobby, remembering the time she and Tilly had come to New York in high school to see the Christmas tree at Rockefeller

Center and had ducked into the Plaza, just to see what it was like. As far as she could see, it hadn't changed much.

"Might I ask," she said to the man behind the counter, "how much a room in this place costs?"

He told her how much her room would have cost her. *Was* costing someone else. Patience had a damned good idea who that someone was.

She managed not to choke. She had just enough cash to cover the tab, but she would have had to break out the plastic to eat. Her New Year's resolution had been to send her credit cards back to their appropriate banks in small pieces.

Pride had never gotten in the way of a Madrid and a free meal, never mind a free night in Manhattan. They were a practical lot. They also never judged their self-worth or anyone else's by the size of their bank accounts.

She got her room assignment and key and thanked the man who'd introduced himself as Frank.

Patience carried her own bag up to her room.

It had no view and she'd hate to figure out what it was costing Jake Putnam Farr per square foot. But it was the Plaza, elegant, unique, hard not to appreciate.

She called her sister's apartment. Jake answered on the fourth ring; she hadn't realized that she'd counted. "What if I told you I don't accept charity?"

"I'd say fine, you're on your own."

"You wouldn't argue with me?"

"No."

"You wouldn't make me feel like I couldn't get along without you?"

"Well, I'd like to think you can't," he said, his voice low, deliberately sexy, "but not because of money."

She refused to let him think he'd gotten to her, although he had. "You're worth a lot?"

"I'm used to paying New York prices."

She wasn't. In fact, she hated to part with a nickel. Frugality was a way of life for her, a choice more than a necessity, although she suspected environmental writing didn't pay as well as management consulting or whatever it was Jake Farr did for a living. Not much, so far as she could see. And it wasn't just New York prices he was used to. It was his New York lifestyle.

"Who's Emmie Dalton?" she asked.

"The travel agent friend who told me where your sister and Terrence are staying."

"Oh. Think she can find out what room they're in? I don't think hotel security would take to my peeking in keyholes. Hate to have Tilly need to haul me out of jail."

"I can ask, but I've called in all my chips with her—"

"Then it's okay. I wouldn't want to put you on the spot. I'll figure out something."

He grumbled something she couldn't make out.

"You okay?" she asked.

"Yes. It's this dog of yours. He insists on climbing in bed with me."

"You're in bed?"

"With a book, yes. But *The Three Musketeers* is no match for what I had in mind before you decided to spend the night at the Plaza."

She felt a rush of heat in a few strategic places, reminding her of how easily she reacted physically to Jake Putnam Farr. It had nothing to do with common sense. It wasn't even anything she could control. She could control what she *did* about it—getting into bed with him, for instance—but not its existence. It was so damned complicated, and yet, in its essence, so very simple. She wanted to make love to him. Wanted him to make love to her.

"Patience, are you there?"

She cleared her throat. "Mmm, yes."

"Sleep well," he murmured.

Now that, she thought as she hung up, would be a trick.

10

"I'M SORRY," the woman at the front desk said, "we have no one at all registered under the name Terwilliger."

Hunching her shoulder to hold the phone, Patience tucked her feet under the covers of her Plaza Hotel bed. So far, she'd drawn a blank with Terrence and Matilda Terwilliger or any combination of names ending with Terwilliger.

"What about Madrid?" she asked.

"First name?"

She leaned forward anxiously. "Matilda or Tilly."

"I'm sorry, no."

Damn! "Patience. You do—"

"Yes, ma'am, I am trying to be patient."

"No, no, I'm not criticizing you. I'm just making sure you do have a Patience Madrid registered."

A short pause. "Let me see . . . yes. I do have a Patience Madrid registered. I had no idea . . . it's an unusual name."

"I'll agree with you there since I've put up with it for thirty-two years. Look—" But she hesitated. There'd been something about the woman's tone. Patience took the receiver in one hand and pulled the blankets up over her knees. She'd ordered a bottle of very expensive champagne—Jake Farr would learn not to be so generous. Not one to waste anything, she'd already drunk two glasses herself. But she was feeling sleepy now. Possibly she'd just imagined hearing something in the woman's tone.

Then it hit her—why had she needed a *first* name?

Because there was more than one Madrid registered.

If not Tilly, who?

"Is there a Sarah or Jebediah Madrid registered?"

"I'm sorry, no."

Those were the names of her parents. Patience considered. "Isaiah Madrid?"

The woman on the other end was silent. "Miss Madrid, I'm not sure I should reveal—"

"So good ol' Uncle Isaiah *is* here! Terrific." She had to think fast. "Can you connect me to his room? Gosh, it's been years. We're having a family reunion here in New York, you know, and I just wasn't sure who all was coming and staying at the Plaza. Well, it's been confusing, but you can understand."

"Yes," she said dubiously, "I suppose I can. I'll put you through."

Isaiah Madrid.

When she got hold of her sister . . .

But after two rings, she hung up.

This was too easy. Not on her. On *them*.

Her hands were shaking. The Hidden Camel, the Hidden Flamingo, depression, Jake Putnam Farr. Her

sister and brother-in-law had put her through a lot.
They'd taken advantage of her. Made assumptions
about her and the life she'd led.

They'd put her in one hell of a spot. She wanted revenge.

She called the Terwilligers' apartment on the west
side of the park. The phone rang and rang and rang,
but there was no answer. She hung up, wondering if
she'd dialed the right number. She was feeling the effects of the champagne. Her eyelids heavy, she tried
once more.

Still no answer.

Were the two Jakes out for an evening walk? Had
Jake Farr decided he'd had a big enough dose of the
Madrid family and retreated to his own apartment?
Just abandoned dog and cats and headed home?

She wouldn't blame him.

Restless and a little dopey, Patience jumped out of
bed and marched into the bathroom. Turning on the
water good and hot, she filled the tub. The hell with
"Mr. and Mrs. Isaiah Madrid." The hell with Jake
Putnam Farr. How often did she get to spend a night
in a fancy hotel on someone's else's tab? She didn't
have a bathtub in the mountains. She added some
bath oil she'd scrounged from room service. Lord only
knew how much it'd cost Jake. Served him right, too,
although she didn't know why she was mad at *him*.

She'd soak, think, get a good night's sleep, and in
the morning she'd deal with her sister, her brother-in-
law and maybe even Jake Farr.

Before she climbed into the tub, she tried him one more time.

Zip.

What if he'd been manipulated by Tilly again? What if she'd called him with another wild tale about her lunatic sister and he'd swallowed every word?

"You're getting paranoid," she said aloud.

And why not? Wasn't she seven floors up in one of New York City's ritziest hotels hunting for her sister who was registered under their dead uncle's name?

She poured herself another glass of champagne, shut the bathroom door, locked it and climbed into the tub, easing herself into the steaming, fragrant water. She sipped from the glass.

"Just think," she said aloud. "I could be home cutting snarls out of Jake's fur."

Life in New York among the Farrs and Terwilligers could be confusing, she thought, leaning back, but it did have its moments.

TERRENCE TERWILLIGER III climbed into the cab Jake had taken from Central Park West and was now parked in front of the Plaza. The dog was flopped between them. Dressed in an elegant evening suit, Terrence eyed the hound with distaste. "Good dog," he said dubiously.

"Patience says you don't like him."

"How astute of her."

"I didn't want to leave him alone too long in the apartment with your cats."

"Matilda's cats," Terrence corrected dryly, his tolerance on a low ebb. "How the devil did we get mixed up with the Madrid family?"

"Fate, I think."

"Maybe someone put a curse on us back in nursery school."

"Were they born then?"

"Doesn't matter. Had to have been a witch that thought them up."

Jake smiled. In spite of Terrence's dark words, the man was plainly and hopelessly in love with his wife. Jake had just witnessed them walking hand in hand into the Plaza Hotel like a couple of dewy-eyed kids. It was obvious their marriage was *not* in trouble. If Jake could be sure of anything about the past few days, he could be certain of that.

"I thought for a minute you hadn't seen me," Jake said.

"Recognized the dog."

It wasn't a point of pride for Terrence. He did not like his sister-in-law's dog and seemed not at all pleased to have spotted him outside the Plaza Hotel. Patience Madrid was obviously a lot more than Terrence Terwilliger was used to dealing with. As for her dog, the cab driver had agreed to let him come along on the grounds a window was kept open. It had been a chilly ride. Naturally the homely beast had enjoyed every minute of it, keeping his head poked out the entire way.

"I put Matilda on the elevator and told her I thought I'd seen a business associate and wanted to say hello," Terrence said, unusually formal. "I don't normally lie, but this time..." He exhaled, loosening his tie. "Jake, what the hell's going on?"

The question of the hour. "I was hoping you'd tell me."

Terrence shook his head. "All I know is Matilda made plans for us to go to Florida and we ended up staying in New York. She said it was a surprise. Then she had me call you about her sister." He squinted at Jake. "*Is* she depressed?"

"No."

"I didn't think so. Depression...well, it's just not a state of mind I associate with Patience. She has her ups and downs like anyone else—she just handles them differently."

"What about recently?"

"I haven't seen her in ages. I know she's had a hard winter, workwise. Several deadlines in a row, that sort of thing, but it was my understanding that she was thriving up north in that cabin of hers...until Matilda told me otherwise."

"Terrence," Jake said carefully, "has it occurred to you that you and I might be the victims of your wife's little scheme to get your sister-in-law and me together?"

"What do you mean?"

Although Jake thought his friend already knew, he said, "Matilda's been playing matchmaker."

Terrence winced. "But isn't this awfully elaborate?
Telling me we were going to Florida, then having us
stay here in New York, calling you about Patience being depressed.... Really, it's a bit much."

"You haven't heard the half of it. Tilly—Matilda
also led Patience to believe your marriage was on the
skids."

At that, Terrence laughed, incredulous.

"That's how she got her to come to New York and
take care of the cats in the first place," Jake went on.
"And as for the Florida ruse, she must have known
Patience would come after her once she figured out
what was going on." He paused. "And she was right."

Terrence paled, his worst suspicions confirmed.
"You mean Patience is *here?*"

"Here and loaded for bear, Terrence."

"But this is all so...so ridiculous. For heaven's sake,
Jake, you were supposed to be out of town this week.
Who could have predicted your mountain-climbing
trip would fall through? It was a coincidence."

Jake looked at his longtime friend. "Was it?"

The dog shifted between them as Terrence thought
for a moment. Then he said, ominously, "Emmie
Dalton."

"Bingo."

Taking a few minutes to digest the likelihood that
he'd been had by the woman in his life, Terrence finally turned back to his friend. "What now?"

"I haven't the faintest idea."

Terrence patted his sister-in-law's dog. "Those Madrid sisters are quite a pair."

"I agree," Jake said. "But in this case I'd say Patience is Matilda's unwitting victim."

"Perhaps, but she was due."

"What do you mean?"

"I've never told you how Matilda and I met, have I?" But before Jake could answer, Terrence leaned over the front seat and spoke to the cabbie. "Drive—my friend and I need to talk. Take us down Fifth Avenue to the Museum of Fine Arts and back, will you?"

"Just keep the window open."

As the cab pulled away from the curb, the dog lunged onto Terrence's lap and stuck his hairy head out the window, his ears pinned back in the wind, dog slobber flying. Terrence gave the beast room.

"You'd think Patience could have come up with a different name," he said. "But she knew what she was doing."

Jake stiffened. "What do you mean?"

Terrence rubbed his jaw, clearly ill at ease. "That's another story you don't know about—and I'm not sure if I should tell you. If you tell Matilda . . ."

"I won't."

Jake understood his friend's strong penchant for privacy. It had led some—including, apparently, his own sister-in-law—to think he was something of a stuffed shirt.

Terrence reluctantly began to talk.

HER SKIN HAD BEGUN to shrivel and wrinkle, and Patience knew if she didn't haul herself out of the tub soon she'd fall asleep and drown. She'd finished her third glass of champagne.

Yawning, she decided her revenge plot could wait until morning. She needed sleep.

But as she flicked the drain open with her toe, she heard a commotion in her room and shot up straight, instantly alert.

Nothing. Just silence.

Had she imagined an intrusion? No one could have gotten into her room. She'd latched the chain lock.

Hadn't she?

"I can't remember," she whispered, feeling a stab of panic.

Without a sound—unless the whole damned building could hear her heart pounding—she carefully climbed out of the tub. She'd left her clothes in the outer room. Why be modest when she was supposed to be alone? Without bothering to dry off, she wrapped up in the terrycloth robe the hotel provided.

Still nothing from the outer room.

Was she getting paranoid?

She pressed her ear to the bathroom door, held her breath and listened.

There was a distinctly male grunt. And panting. She was sure of it. It sounded canine to her, but how would a dog get into the Plaza Hotel?

Then, *"Dom Pérignon!"*

It was an angry bellow from a man who perhaps wasn't as accustomed to high New York living as she liked to believe.

"Jake? Jake Farr, is that you?"

Jake the dog barked.

"Quiet," the other Jake said, "before you get us all tossed."

She could hear footsteps.

Then, close to the bathroom door, Jake Farr said seductively, "Hello, Patience. I see you've been having quite an evening for yourself. Why didn't you order caviar to go with your champagne?"

"Wish I'd thought of it." Her heart was pounding even faster than when she'd thought he was a mere burglar. And the rush in her head was not the alcohol. "What're you doing here?"

"I had nightmares someone was spending all my money."

She grinned. "Thought you were used to New York prices."

"Dom Pérignon is expensive wherever you go. You could've exercised some restraint, you know."

"I did."

"How?"

She pulled open the door. "I could have ordered *two* bottles of champagne."

Jake was standing on the threshold, barring the door with his solid, masculine body, devastingly handsome in jeans and a deep burgundy shirt. Deeply aware of her own near-nakedness, Patience noticed his dark, probing eyes. He inhaled.

"Evening," she said and hiccuped.

He slowly let out his breath. "Good thing you didn't order that second bottle."

"Guess you shouldn't have bragged about the size of your bank account—"

"I didn't."

She shrugged. "It was implied bragging."

"There's no such thing. You should be grateful, you know. I know you'd never admit it, but you'd never have gotten a room without my help. Emmie had to pull strings."

"Listen here, Jake Putnam Farr, nothing—not the price or availability of a room at the Plaza Hotel— *nothing* would keep me from tracking down my sister once I'd put my mind to it."

Jake's eyes didn't quaver. "No doubt."

She thrust her hands onto her hips. "Are you patronizing me?"

"Wouldn't dream of it."

His voice was mild and, as far as she could tell, perfectly sincere. But, as he stood with his gaze upon her, she had the distinct impression that he wasn't really paying attention to their conversation. Suddenly self-conscious, Patience felt water dripping from her hair, down her neck and between her breasts. She felt the moistness between her legs. She felt dizzy.

"I need to get a towel . . ."

His gaze lingered where the droplets of water gleamed at her cleavage.

Intensely aware of her every move, she grabbed a folded towel, patted dry her face and toweled her hair. Jake didn't move from the doorway. He wasn't menacing or leering or anything like that. He was just *there*. And that, for Patience, was enough.

"How'd you get Jake in?" she asked to break the silence.

"I bribed a bellhop—cost me a pair of hockey tickets." The dog chose that moment to squeeze into the bathroom and drink from the toilet. "I had considered leaving him at your sister's for the night."

Patience swung around. "For the *night?* Jake—"

"It was lonely in that big apartment with just me and Jake and the cats."

He didn't sound lonely. He sounded like he was making a lame excuse. His grin said he wasn't trying too hard. Patience hung up the towel and followed her dog out of the bathroom. The air in the outer room felt cool on her overheated skin and helped to clear her fuzzy head.

"Besides," Jake said, "I didn't know how you'd take to being without your dog for a whole night in the big city."

She turned to look at him. "Jake Farr, are you serious?"

He laughed. "No."

"Then why are you here?"

His grin fading, he moved toward her. "Why do you think?"

"To be honest, I don't know—"

"Don't you?"

He was close enough now that she could see the fine lines at the corners of his eyes and the few gray strands in his dark hair. He was close enough that she could smell the heady cologne she'd found in his shaving kit when she'd thought he and Tilly. . . .

It seemed so silly now, what she'd thought. Tilly would never have an affair. If she and Terrence were having problems, Tilly would confront Terrence about them. She was like Patience in that one way— not afraid of confrontation.

No, confrontation is easy compared to this. Compared to telling a man that you think you're falling for him . . . that you're afraid you already have.

She exhaled, trying to smile. "I know it's been a strange week—"

"Patience." He moved even closer, placing his palms gently on her shoulders. "Patience, if you want me to leave, I'll leave."

"No, it's not that. There're two beds—"

"Patience," he said.

"Did you come here just because . . . just to . . ."

He sighed. "Let's say you are definitely on my mind."

"But?"

"They're on the tenth floor. I've got the room number written down here somewhere."

She grinned. "You're kidding! Emmie Dalton again? You'll have to thank her for me. And thank *you*, Jake. I know you must think this is weird, but Tilly and I— well, I just have to put my mind at ease that she's not crazy."

"I understand," he said.

But there was something about his expression. If the champagne hadn't dulled her wits, she might have been able to discern what it was. "Jake, are you all right? Is there something else you need to tell me?"

"No."

"Look, I know Tilly and I must seem as different as night and day. Most people probably do think our lives have drifted apart, that we don't have as much in common as we once did. But that's not what's going on here. It's something else. Tilly and I are sisters, Jake. We'll always be sisters. If I'm worried it's because I have cause to be worried."

"I'm beginning to see," he said carefully, "that you and your sister have a hell of a lot more in common than I'd ever have believed."

"Because of whatever scam she's got going on me? The Hidden Flamingo, the Hidden Camel. And now the Plaza Hotel..." Patience laughed languidly. "What do you suppose she could be up to?"

"Whatever it is, it can wait until morning. Fiery though your soul may yet be, Miss Madrid, you look about done in. It's been a long day."

"It really has."

And when they turned around, Jake—the big black, hairy one—had made himself at home in the middle of the second bed. Patience had taken the one near the window.

"You scroungy dog," Jake said. "Off the bed."

Jake didn't budge.

"He probably blames you for getting him dunked," Patience said.

"Me? It wasn't my fault. The stupid mutt . . . Come on, off the bed."

Jake yawned and stretched out his long, bony legs.

"You've spoiled him," Patience said. "You should never have fed him from the table. Now he won't do anything you say."

"Then *you* get him off my bed."

"What makes you think that one's your bed?"

"Because you've already camped out in the other one."

"But I thought you came here for—"

He looked at her, and his eyes, usually so dark and impenetrable, were shining, tender, an open door to his soul. "I came here for what you want, for what you're ready for," he said softly. "Nothing more."

"That's it?" she asked. Her voice, too, was soft, and she wondered if her eyes were as affectionate and trusting. She wanted this man to know her. To like her for who she really was.

"And just to be with you," he said simply. "We're allies, soul mates in this little venture." His eyes narrowed a little, betraying just that hint of suspicion she'd detected earlier. But suspicion of what? "You *have* told me everything, haven't you?"

"About Tilly and Terrence? Yes—yes, I have."

He smiled, but the hint of suspicion was still there.

"Jake, is something on your mind?"

"Oh, yes." And the suspicion vanished, so quickly Patience wasn't sure she hadn't just imagined it. It was replaced by a devilish grin and a low laugh, as he scooped her against him with one arm. "There's definitely something on my mind."

She pretended not to understand. "What? You know you can tell me anything."

He lowered his mouth close to hers, so that their breath mingled.

"What do you want to hear?" he asked.

"Whatever you want to say."

"I want to say..." he paused, licking his lower lip, his tongue almost touching her mouth "...I want to make love to you, Patience Madrid."

For a moment, she was lost for words. Then she murmured, "I thought that's what you might say."

He didn't back down. "It's the truth."

She nodded, slipping her hands around his waist, locking her fingers at the small of his back. Their bodies fit together so well. They might have been made for each other, except Patience didn't think like that. Love was too special for her to believe she and Jake didn't have anything to do with where they were, how they were feeling, at this moment. It was too easy to say it was destiny. It made what she was feeling right now—a mixture of passion and a desire to love and be loved—seem trivial, outside her control. As if what she and Jake did, who they were, didn't matter.

But all that *did* matter. Love wasn't just about bells and whistles going off that first moment two people destined for each other met. The only bells and whistles likely to have gone off when Patience saw Jake Farr being thrown back against the elevator by her big dog were alarms and sirens.

Was she in love with him?

"Jake's had a rough day," she whispered, and they both knew she meant her dog. "Let's let him have the other bed. If he wrecks the bedspread, I'll reimburse the Plaza myself."

"Are you sure?"

"Oh, yes. How expensive can a bedspread be?"

He tightened his grip on her. "Not about the damned dog, Patience. About *us*."

She smiled. "I know what you meant. I was just..." She stopped, realizing this wasn't the time for teasing. "Yes—yes, Jake, I'm sure." Her hands drifted up his back, and she pressed herself against him, the robe falling open. "Thank you for asking."

It was the last thing she said before his mouth captured hers.

Her robe dropped to the floor.

She could feel that his breath had stopped. She drew herself against him, until his hands drifted down her spine and caught the curve of her hips. She gave a small gasp.

He smiled against her mouth. "I'd given up on finding someone like you."

"I'm not sure I ever dared hope I'd find you."

His eyes sparkled, his hands smoothing lower, down her bottom, to the tops of her thighs,. "I thought you weren't afraid of anything."

Slowly, erotically, one hand slipped between his body and hers, between her legs.

Now her breath stopped.

"Everybody's afraid of something," she whispered.

Her thighs parted and his fingers touched her hot, moist center.

His mouth found hers again, and she responded immediately, eagerly, her tongue matching the erotic, primitive rhythm of his. He kissed her chin, her throat, igniting her. He bent his head and his tongue flicked against one hardened nipple, then the other, then back again, until she moaned, aroused and excited. Between her legs, his fingers moved deeper, until she moved against them, responding.

She could hear his sharp, tortured intake of breath.

Then he pulled away and began tearing off clothes. His shirt, his pants, his underclothes. He moved fast, unselfconsciously, unblushingly. Patience watched. He caught her and grinned. In a moment, he was naked. Magnificently naked. Solid, sleek, muscled.

They fell together on the big hotel bed, kissing each other, exploring, exulting in the passion they shared, until finally she was on top of him and he was lifting her, and she knew it was time. Every fiber of her body and being wanted him.

"Patience," he breathed, "oh, Patience."

She murmured his name and felt him come into her. She heard his soft, welcoming groan as he wrapped his arms around her and she drew him deeper into her.

She couldn't speak, couldn't make a sound.

Then the control disappeared. Where there had been a quiet, romantic fire now there was a conflagration, hot flames erupting all around them. Patience thought she would explode.

Together, they rolled over, until she was on her back, knowing only that she wanted more, all of him. He thrust hard and fast, and she realized her fingers were dug into the hard muscles of his thighs. She wanted more heat. More fire. More explosions.

And when the final one came, it rocked her to her very soul.

There had never been anyone remotely like Jake Putnam Farr in her life. He was the spark that set her ablaze. Together they were unstoppable, a flame that no one—nothing—could extinguish.

Or so it was in the darkness of the New York night, when Jake was with her. Right now the mountains, where she'd always felt she belonged, were far away. Come morning, she just didn't know where she'd feel she belonged. Anywhere so long as it was with Jake Farr? But that was too easy, and life, she knew, just wasn't that easy.

He held her, kissed her gently. "Good night, Patience Madrid. Sleep well."

Laying her head against his shoulder, she knew she'd be lucky to sleep at all.

A LONG TIME LATER, she became aware that he, too, was still awake. She raised herself up and looked down at him, his long, lean figure outlined in the darkness. She touched the long, jagged scar above his right knee. "I noticed this earlier," she said, half-smiling, "but didn't think it exactly the right time to comment."

He trailed one finger down her left thigh, where she had a scar. "Same here."

"One little mistake with a chainsaw. You?"

"Mountain-climbing in the Alps. Were you alone?"

"Yes."

"You're lucky you didn't bleed to death."

"Uncle Isaiah was still alive then. He was off fishing or something. He hauled me off to the hospital when he got back, lecturing me the whole way on what I'd done wrong. It's not a mistake I'll ever make again."

"One would hope."

"How'd you manage in the mountains?"

"I had a friend with me."

"Terrence?"

"Yes. He hadn't met your sister yet. He patched me up and went for help."

"You're good friends, aren't you?"

There was no hesitation. "Yes."

She smiled and kissed his scar.

When she finished, he kissed hers, and it was a long time again before, at last, they slept.

11

PATIENCE WAS UP EARLY. She showered, got dressed, kicked her dog off the extra bed and ordered room service before Jake even stirred. "Sleeping past sun-up's abnormal," Uncle Isaiah used to say. For a long time Patience had believed him. Now she believed in tolerance.

But it *was* getting late. Almost eight o'clock. She hoped a newspaper would come with her breakfast. Usually by now she knew what was going on in the world.

She considered putting Jake up to licking his new friend's face, but decided that was mean. After last night, the man needed his sleep. So did Patience. Habit and a guilty conscience had gotten her up earlier than her body had wanted.

She had a fair idea that Jake Farr had figured out she hadn't quite told him everything about Tilly's little matchmaking scheme. Like that Patience might know her sister's motive for doing it.

There was a quiet knock at the door. Expecting room service, Patience opened it up. She was shocked to see her sister standing on the threshold in a designer pantsuit.

"Tilly, how in the world did you know I was here?" she blurted out.

She brushed off her younger sister's question. "That's the least of your worries right now. Patience, you're not going to believe—"

Patience quickly shushed her. "No, Til, *you're* not going to believe." Looking behind her, she saw that Jake Farr was still sound asleep. She scooted out the door. "I've got company."

"Who?"

"Don't be an idiot, Tilly."

"You mean *Jake?*"

"Both Jakes."

"Oh, my..." Tilly shook her head, looking a bit pale. "If I get out of this alive, I'm going to pretend I've never heard of either of you."

"A little late for that, don't you think?"

"You weren't supposed to fall for the guy!"

Patience frowned, unwilling to discuss her love life, even with her sister, in the seventh floor hall of the Plaza Hotel.

Tilly sighed. She was an attractive woman, shorter and more fine-boned than Patience, less prone these days to wielding an ax. Her hair was a more demure shade of red, and her two-hundred-dollar cuts had it nicely tamed. Her nails were painted a pretty coral, and Patience knew for a fact she didn't have any chainsaw scars on her. But she was Uncle Isaiah's niece, Sarah and Jebediah Madrid's older daughter. She was not all Terwilliger.

"Terrence is onto me," she announced.

"So I guess this means that he wasn't in on your little scheme. It must have been a surprise when he thought he was going to Florida and ended up around the corner from where he lives in the Big Apple."

"I wouldn't be sarcastic if I were you. Did your buddy in there tell you he saw Terrence last night?"

Patience felt her own face lose its color.

"There," Tilly said, not particularly enjoying her small victory. "See? We should have listened to Uncle Isaiah and never gotten ourselves mixed up with New York men."

"Meeting Jake wasn't my idea."

Tilly's eyes—as teal as her younger sister's—flashed. "Don't tell me you didn't know I'd have my revenge one of these days, Patience Madrid. *You* started this."

She bit her lip, knowing she had.

"I saw Jake Farr and your damned dog in a cab outside the Plaza last night. Terrence brushed me off. He thought I didn't know what was going on, but he's the worst liar. I looked out the window and saw him getting into the cab. He and Farr must have had a good long talk. They..." She shrugged. "Well, they obviously will look upon themselves as victims in this whole thing."

"They would," Patience said.

"We have to do something."

"Like what?"

Obviously Tilly didn't have the faintest idea.

"How'd you find me?" Patience asked.

"Emmie Dalton. I called the rat fink after I saw Terrence and Jake together. She confessed everything and said we all owed her for putting her on the spot the way we did. I guess she has a point." She chewed her lower lip. "Well, what're we going to do?"

"We're Madrids, Til. What do we always do in a crisis?"

She looked at her sister. Then the panic faded, and she smiled. "Wing it."

JAKE AWOKE to the delivery of the most enormous breakfast he'd ever seen. There were also two messages for him. The first was in the form of a scrap of a note in Patience's distinctive scrawl: "I'm walking Jake. Enjoy your breakfast. Hope you're hungry." He had to call downstairs for the second message.

"There's a note here from Mr. Terwilliger," the woman at the front desk said.

"Can you read it to me?"

"Certainly. 'Jake: I'll be getting Matilda out of the picture today as planned. Is Paris far enough?'"

Jake laughed. "Thanks."

He turned to the breakfast tray. Patience Madrid was not shy about her appetite. She'd ordered eggs, yogurt, a basket of muffins and sweet rolls, fresh fruit, a pot of coffee and—a bottle of champagne. Not, he noted, Dom Pérignon. Still, he could have eaten for a week on what that one breakfast cost.

He poured himself a cup of coffee and contemplated the fate of the Madrid sisters.

Ahh, sweet revenge.

Patience returned a few minutes later, red-faced and out of breath, her dog panting beside her. "We've been asked to leave."

"Got caught, did you?"

"I guess I don't have your gift for having my way in the big city." She pushed back her wild hair. She'd dressed in her stirrups and Norwegian wool sweater. At least she'd left her dead uncle's shirt up in the woods. "I've got fifteen minutes to pack up me and my dog and hit the road. How's breakfast?"

"There's enough here to feed half the hotel."

"One would hope—it cost a fortune."

Jake judiciously withheld comment. He swallowed a bite of blueberry muffin as he stood at the window. Patience whirled around their room, throwing her things together and grumbling at Jake— they'd really have to come up with another name for that beast—for being so obtuse as to try to make friends with a woman wearing *that* many diamonds. Jake didn't ask how many. She'd gone into her salt-of-the-earth mode and only would fuss at him for having money, which he did and wasn't about to pretend he didn't.

Carefully, he watched the street below. Then suddenly there they were. He stiffened with the incipient thrill of victory.

"Patience," he said, "come here a minute. I think I see your sister."

"What? Are you serious?"

She raced to the window and peered down, frowning when she spotted Terrence and Matilda Terwilliger climbing into a cab. Jake noted that Terrence took his time, making sure anyone watching from up above would get a good look at his wife.

"Where do you suppose they're going?" Jake asked mildly.

"Could be just out shopping."

But a bellhop came out and put the Terwilligers' luggage into the trunk of the cab.

"They're leaving!"

She started for the door, but Jake grabbed her by the elbow, stopping her in her conspiratorial tracks. "You'll never make it in time."

"But I promised—I told Tilly I wouldn't abandon her to Terrence and . . ."

Jake was enjoying himself. Oh, but he did like knowing what was going on. "You told Tilly, did you? What and when exactly did you tell her?"

Patience bit her lip. He could see she knew she'd blown it.

"Patience?"

Her beautiful teal eyes fastened on him. He refused to be swayed into feeling any pity. The Madrid sisters had this coming. If anyone should be pitied, Jake thought, it was Terrence and himself.

Of course, after last night . . .

"How much do you know?" she asked.

"Everything."

Freeing her arm, she walked over to the breakfast tray and poured herself a cup of coffee and popped a chunk of fresh pineapple into her mouth. He admired her calm. The woman did have a certain way of handling the unexpected.

"Where's Terrence taking my sister?"

"Paris."

She nodded. "I'd have thought a desert island."

"I'm sure it's something he considered, but since he's going with her, he didn't want to have to suffer."

"Is he mad at her?"

"Let's just say he's been waiting for the other shoe to drop for more than a year."

He thought he saw Patience's calm falter. Apparently when he'd said "everything" she didn't expect he meant *everything*. But he did.

She cleared her throat. "Um—I guess I don't know what to say."

Jake wondered if that was a first. "It didn't occur to you that Tilly was getting her revenge?"

"Not soon enough. I figured since she and Terrence ended up getting married that she'd let bygones be bygones and wouldn't come after me." She ate a couple of grapes. "And I guess when she indicated she and Terrence were having marital problems I blamed myself, so my guard went down. I fell for her scheme hook, line and sinker."

So had Jake. Only he had been at a great disadvantage. He hadn't known—as everyone else involved had—the true circumstances of how Terrence Terwilliger and Matilda Madrid had met.

"You picked Terrence's name out of the *Wall Street Journal?*"

Patience nodded. If she had any regrets, Jake couldn't see a sign of them in her matter-of-fact expression. It was as if she set people up every day. "It was in an announcement of promotions at his firm. I mean, Terrence Terwilliger III? How could I resist?"

Jake chose not to answer. Of course she hadn't resisted. She'd made up some fake stationery on her expensive computer in the mountains and dashed off a letter, ostensibly from Terrence, to her sister threatening to sue her on some specious grounds. One thing had led to another.

"I thought 'Tilly Terwilliger' sounded so ridiculous that one or the other of them would catch on before anything happened."

"Like their getting married."

"Precisely."

"So when Tilly implied she and Terrence were having problems, you were quick to blame yourself for ever having 'introduced' them."

Sinking onto the edge of the bed, she exhaled. "They're so different. Of course, Tilly—she's no dummy, you know—she counted on guilt to keep me from getting suspicious."

"It worked," Jake pointed out, walking over and sitting down beside her. Life with the Madrid sisters, Terrence had said, was never dull. Jake thought he knew what he meant.

"Terrence vowed he'd never tell a soul."

"He finally had to—we *are* friends, you know."

"Are you mad?"

"At your sister? No. She owed me, too, you know. I played a practical joke on her last Christmas and she promised revenge. I never thought she'd throw me to her little sister." He grinned. "But I think I handled it."

He thought he saw Patience shiver. "What now?" she said.

"Well, Terrence has seen to it your sister's out of the way." Jake leaned over for the coffeepot and poured himself another cup. "You and your hairy mutt have been thrown out of the Plaza Hotel. We've got two neglected cats back on Central Park West."

"So it's back to normal."

"No, I wouldn't say that. I don't think we'll ever go back to where we were before my elevator hit the lobby on Saturday morning. We'll have to fashion a new normal for ourselves."

"Jake—"

"It's just us now, Patience. You and me and your critters. The question is, what're *you* going to do?"

WHAT PATIENCE DID was fall in love with Jake Putnam Farr.

Terrence kept Tilly out of New York for three more weeks. Patience received postcards from Paris, then Rome, then Vienna, Copenhagen, Amsterdam. They all begged Patience to be patient and tend her cats. They all sounded like Terrence's idea of revenge suited Tilly fine.

Patience took care of Apollo and Aphrodite. They even became friends of sorts. Aphrodite developed a taste for beer. Apollo learned to fetch, which was more than Jake had ever done. All the animals learned to stay out of the bedroom when Jake Farr was in it. Not Patience, however. She was in Jake Farr's bedroom every night. It wasn't really *his*, she'd point out, nor hers, nor theirs.

They did not, it became painfully obvious, have a place of their own.

She resumed working. So, to her mild surprise, did he. Evenings they went to dinner or cooked together. They saw shows and hockey games and movies and walked through Central Park hand in hand. They had long talks about politics and the economy and philosophy and romance and the environment. They argued. They made love. Patience was convinced she would never get enough of him. Every time they were together seemed more remarkable—more transforming—than the last. There was always more to discover, always more to give.

And then it was time for Patience to head back to the mountains. Just like that. Terrence and Tilly were coming home.

And so it was on the first day of April that Patience woke up all alone on Uncle Isaiah's old horsehair mattress. She built a fire to take the chill out of the air. Then let Jake out. Got into her exercise clothes and went for a fast, hard walk around the lake, trying to get back into the spirit of her isolated existence.

"I can't come," Jake had told her.

He'd been honest, at least. He had an important business meeting in the city. He had to meet with his architect. His architect for *his* apartment. Just as it was *her* log cabin.

Did whatever they had together necessitate separate lives?

Did he need to keep his apartment, she her cabin?

She walked faster, harder, her lungs burning, the mud squishing under her sneakers. Four days she'd been back. There'd been an enraged phone call from Tilly about Aphrodite's sudden interest in beer, but nothing from Jake. Nor had Patience called him. Perhaps they needed to know what it was they had apart in order to better understand what it was they had together.

Then again, Jake Farr was independent, a man accustomed to keeping his own company, having his own space. Patience understood. They weren't, she thought, as different as her sister had thought when she'd set them up.

At the end of her walk, she did a few stretches out on the dock and threw rocks in the water, smiling at the memory of Jake Farr going head over heels into the frigid lake.

In the distance, she could hear the engine of an approaching vehicle. Her heart pounded. It was still too early for tourists. Jake?

She raced up to her cabin, only to see a delivery truck backing into her driveway. She ran up to him. "I'm sorry, but you must have the wrong house—"

"You're Patience Madrid, aren't you?"

The burly man looked confident that she was, and she nodded as he climbed out of the truck. "What do you have?" she asked.

But he was working, obviously not one for chitchat, and opened the back of the truck and slid out a new mattress and box spring.

"I didn't order a mattress!"

"It's paid for," the man said. "Where do you want me to put it?"

Clearly he was going to leave her with his cargo whether she wanted it or not. She pointed to the porch. With remarkably little effort, he hauled the mattress and then the box spring out of the truck, up the steps and leaned them against the porch rail. They were at least queen-size.

She signed on the line the man indicated, and he departed.

She scratched Jake's head. "Well, what're we going to do with a new bed?"

"I hope by *we*," Jake Farr said behind her, "you mean you and me, not you and him."

Startled, she swung around, and Jake walked down from the driveway. With the loud truck, she hadn't heard his car. The sunlight seemed to dance on his dark hair, in his dark eyes. It was a bright, warm day, and he'd just worn a pullover and jeans. She felt a rush of emotion. Tears sprang to her eyes. That had never happened to her. She was Patience Madrid. The mountain woman. The hard case who could damned well take care of herself. But she also knew now that she didn't have to prove that to anyone—herself and Jake Farr included.

"Jake . . ."

"Do you mean me or that scroungy hound?"

"You. I'm training him to go by a different name."

His eyes narrowed suspiciously. "What?"

"Zeke. It sounds enough like Jake that he's not that confused."

"You don't happen to know a Zeke, do you?"

She shook her head.

He moved closer. "You named that damned dog after me, didn't you?"

"I didn't know you—"

"You might as well fess up." He stood toe-to-toe with her now; they were only inches apart. "You found out Terrence's best friend was named Jake, and when this skinny, ugly hound wandered into your cabin, you couldn't resist. You named him Jake just to irritate your brother-in-law."

"Did he tell you that?"

"Nope."

"Tilly?"

"No, I figured it out all by myself. Terrence warned me this kind of thinking is a direct result of life with a Madrid."

"Well . . ."

He slipped his arms around her waist. "I'm right."

He was right. And he *knew* he was right. So Patience saw no need to tell him.

"If you don't fess up," he said in a low, menacing whisper into her ear, "I am going to toss your pretty behind into the lake."

"Now listen here, Jake Farr, just who do you think you are, extracting confessions from me? I can be stubborn, you know—"

"Oh, I know."

And he picked her up off her feet.

"*Don't you dare!*"

"Confess."

"You can't ask a person to incriminate herself."

He took a few steps toward the lake.

"Jake, I mean it. If you throw me into that water, you'll regret it. I promise you'll regret it—"

Clearly the man wasn't listening. He hoisted her up onto his shoulder like an old rug and hauled her out to the end of the dock.

"Did you or did you not name that dog after me?"

"I'd never even met you."

He sighed. "How cold do you think that water is?"

"Freezing."

"Good."

"Okay, okay," she yelled. "It's true. I named Jake after you. I made . . . certain assumptions about your character."

He didn't say a word. Nor did he lower her back down to the dock.

Then her dog had to join them. He was muddy and slobbery from their trek around the lake and looked even hairier and uglier than usual.

The two Jakes stared at each other. The four-legged one flopped down and started scratching and licking himself. It was a sight.

Patience knew she was doomed. With a low growl, Jake Farr pitched her feetfirst into the lake.

Which was a mistake. Headfirst and she wouldn't have made a quick recovery—the shock of hitting the water would have been too much. But feetfirst she could handle. She hit bottom and popped up like a missile out of a submarine and got him by the leg, knocking him off balance and right into the water with her.

He landed with a yell and a huge splash.

Before he came up for air, she scrambled for shore and beelined for the front porch.

If the damned mattress and box spring hadn't been in the way, she'd have made it. As it was, Jake caught up with her.

"I'm soaked head to toe," she said. "There's nothing you can do to me now."

"Want to make a bet?"

His eyes now blazed with the desire for something other than vengeance, and his grip on her waist softened. Wet and shivering, she smiled and pressed a wet finger to his mouth. "I don't think I'll take that bet."

"Oh, Patience," he breathed.

"I know. Four days—it seems like forever."

"The mattress..." He pushed back his dripping hair. "If you object, I'll send it back. I remember when you said you'd made Uncle Isaiah's place your own by adding a few personal touches. As far as I'm concerned, everything can stay the same—except for that damned horsehair mattress. There, my love, I draw the line."

"Jake—"

He shook his head, not letting her interrupt. "And we have an appointment in New York next week with an interior decorator. I figure neither of us is good at that sort of thing, but I'd like to make my apartment *our* apartment. I want you to add your touches there, too. But if you don't want to live in New York at all, even part-time, it's okay. We'll work something out." He smiled. "I'm talking fast because if I don't I'll freeze to death and then none of this will matter. Patience, I love you. I want to be a part of your life. I want you to be a part of my life. Damn it, if I have to thank your sister for putting us together I will—"

"Jake—oh, Jake." She smiled, feeling warm all of a sudden. "I...I don't know what to say."

"Say you love me."

She laughed. "I love you."

"For all time?"

"And beyond."

"Good." He scooped her up. "Then shall we find out what it's like to warm up on a horsehair mattress?"

WEEKS LATER, on a warm afternoon in early June, Jake met Terrence for lunch at the World Trade Center. They both looked very Wall Street. Dressed in pinstripes, carrying expensive leather briefcases.

Terrence surreptitiously withdrew a flaming orange card from his suitcoat pocket. "Did you get one of these?"

Jake nodded, and withdrew his. He figured Patience had done them up on her computer. She had one in the mountains, one in New York.

"What the hell is it?" Terrence asked.

"It's an invitation to the Madrid family reunion in September."

Terrence shook his head, adamant. "No, please don't say that."

"Then what do you think it is?"

"Do you know how many Madrids there are? Scores, Jake. All of them with names like Patience and Matilda and Jebediah and Isaiah. They're all smart and stubborn and weird. No, this isn't any ordinary family reunion." Terrence's face darkened. "This, my friend, is our wives' revenge."

"You mean they arranged it just to torture us?"

"Oh, yes."

Jake threw back his head and laughed, because he knew Terrence was right. The Madrid sisters always had the last word, and they never gave up.

But, in Terrence Terwilliger III and Jake Putnam Farr, they'd more than met their match.

"Any question of just calling it even?"

"Nope," Jake said, setting down his briefcase. "Not a one."

The two men rolled up their sleeves, and with conversations on the stock market and deficits and bond ratings going on around them, they plotted their next move.

"Think we'll be doing this when we're eighty?" Terrence asked.

Jake had to smile, just thinking of it.

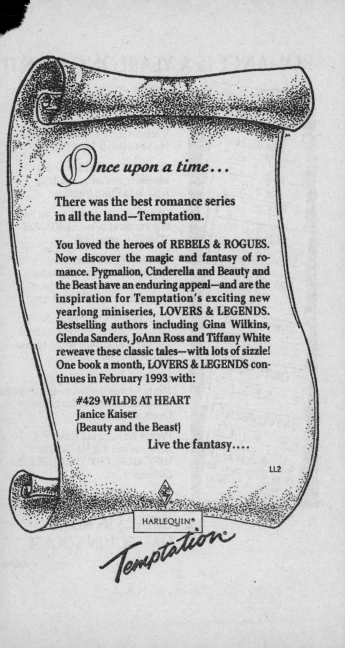

$\mathcal{O}$*nce upon a time...*

There was the best romance series
in all the land—Temptation.

You loved the heroes of REBELS & ROGUES.
Now discover the magic and fantasy of romance. Pygmalion, Cinderella and Beauty and
the Beast have an enduring appeal—and are the
inspiration for Temptation's exciting new
yearlong miniseries, LOVERS & LEGENDS.
Bestselling authors including Gina Wilkins,
Glenda Sanders, JoAnn Ross and Tiffany White
reweave these classic tales—with lots of sizzle!
One book a month, LOVERS & LEGENDS con-
tinues in February 1993 with:

#429 WILDE AT HEART
Janice Kaiser
(Beauty and the Beast)

Live the fantasy....

LL2

HARLEQUIN®

Temptation

ROMANCE IS A YEARLONG EVENT!

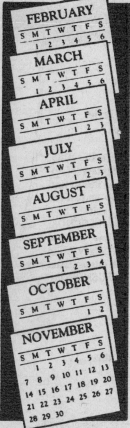

FEBRUARY

S	M	T	W	T	F	S
1	2	3	4	5	6	

MARCH

S	M	T	W	T	F	S
1	2	3	4	5	6	

APRIL

S	M	T	W	T	F	S
					1	2
3						

JULY

S	M	T	W	T	F	S
					1	2
3						

AUGUST

S	M	T	W	T	F	S
						1

SEPTEMBER

S	M	T	W	T	F	S
			1	2	3	4

OCTOBER

S	M	T	W	T	F	S
					1	2

NOVEMBER

S	M	T	W	T	F	S
	1	2	3	4	5	6
7	8	9	10	11	12	13
14	15	16	17	18	19	20
21	22	23	24	25	26	27
28	29	30				

Celebrate the most romantic day of the year with MY VALENTINE! (February)

CRYSTAL CREEK
When you come for a visit Texas-style, you won't want to leave! (March)

Celebrate the joy, excitement and adjustment that comes with being JUST MARRIED! (April)

Go back in time and discover the West as it was meant to be . . . UNTAMED— Maverick Hearts! (July)

LINGERING SHADOWS
New York Times bestselling author Penny Jordan brings you her latest blockbuster. Don't miss it! (August)

BACK BY POPULAR DEMAND!!!
Calloway Corners, involving stories of four sisters coping with family, business and romance! (September)

FRIENDS, FAMILIES, LOVERS
Join us for these heartwarming love stories that evoke memories of family and friends. (October)

Capture the magic and romance of Christmas past with HARLEQUIN HISTORICAL CHRISTMAS STORIES! (November)

WATCH FOR FURTHER DETAILS IN ALL HARLEQUIN BOOKS!

OFFICIAL RULES • MILLION DOLLAR BIG BUCKS SWEEPSTAKES
NO PURCHASE OR OBLIGATION NECESSARY TO ENTER

To enter, follow the directions published. **ALTERNATE MEANS OF ENTRY:** Hand print your name and address on a 3″ × 5″ card and mail to either: Harlequin "Big Bucks," 3010 Walden Ave., P.O. Box 1867, Buffalo, NY 14269-1867, or Harlequin "Big Bucks," P.O. Box 609, Fort Erie, Ontario L2A 5X3, and we will assign your Sweepstakes numbers. (Limit: one entry per envelope.) For eligibility, entries must be received no later than March 31, 1994. No responsibility is assumed for lost, late or misdirected entries.

Upon receipt of entry, Sweepstakes numbers will be assigned. To determine winners, Sweepstakes numbers will be compared against a list of randomly preselected prizewinning numbers. In the event all prizes are not claimed via the return of prizewinning numbers, random drawings will be held from among all other entries received to award unclaimed prizes.

Prizewinners will be determined no later than May 30, 1994. Selection of winning numbers and random drawings are under the supervision of D.L. Blair, Inc., an independent judging organization, whose decisions are final. One prize to a family or organization. No substitution will be made for any prize, except as offered. Taxes and duties on all prizes are the sole responsibility of winners. Winners will be notified by mail. Chances of winning are determined by the number of entries distributed and received.

Sweepstakes open to persons 18 years of age or older, except employees and immediate family members of Torstar Corporation, D.L. Blair, Inc., their affiliates, subsidiaries and all other agencies, entities and persons connected with the use, marketing or conduct of this Sweepstakes. All applicable laws and regulations apply. Sweepstakes offer void wherever prohibited by law. Any litigation within the province of Quebec respecting the conduct and awarding of a prize in this Sweepstakes must be submitted to the Régies des Loteries et Courses du Quebec. In order to win a prize, residents of Canada will be required to correctly answer a time-limited arithmetical skill-testing question. Values of all prizes are in U.S. currency.

Winners of major prizes will be obligated to sign and return an affidavit of eligibility and release of liability within 30 days of notification. In the event of non-compliance within this time period, prize may be awarded to an alternate winner. Any prize or prize notification returned as undeliverable will result in the awarding of that prize to an alternate winner. By acceptance of their prize, winners consent to use of their names, photographs or other likenesses for purposes of advertising, trade and promotion on behalf of Torstar Corporation without further compensation, unless prohibited by law.

This Sweepstakes is presented by Torstar Corporation, its subsidiaries and affiliates in conjunction with book, merchandise and/or product offerings. Prizes are as follows: Grand Prize—$1,000,000 (payable at $33,333.33 a year for 30 years). First through Sixth Prizes may be presented in different creative executions, each with the following approximate values: First Prize—$35,000; Second Prize—$10,000; 2 Third Prizes—$5,000 each; 5 Fourth Prizes—$1,000 each; 10 Fifth Prizes—$250 each; 1,000 Sixth Prizes—$100 each. Prizewinners will have the opportunity of selecting any prize offered for that level. A travel-prize option, if offered and selected by winner, must be completed within 12 months of selection and is subject to hotel and flight accommodations availability. Torstar Corporation may present this Sweepstakes utilizing names other than Million Dollar Sweepstakes. For a current list of all prize options offered within prize levels and all names the Sweepstakes may utilize, send a self-addressed, stamped envelope (WA residents need not affix return postage) to: Million Dollar Sweepstakes Prize Options/Names, P.O. Box 4710, Blair, NE 68009.

The Extra Bonus Prize will be awarded in a random drawing to be conducted no later than May 30, 1994 from among all entries received. To qualify, entries must be received by March 31, 1994 and comply with published directions. No purchase necessary. For complete rules, send a self-addressed, stamped envelope (WA residents need not affix return postage) to: Extra Bonus Prize Rules, P.O. Box 4600, Blair, NE 68009.

For a list of prizewinners (available after July 31, 1994) send a separate, stamped, self-addressed envelope to: Million Dollar Sweepstakes Winners, P.O. Box 4728, Blair, NE 68009.

SWP-H393

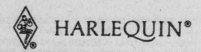

HARLEQUIN®

THE TAGGARTS OF TEXAS!

Harlequin's Ruth Jean Dale brings you
THE TAGGARTS OF TEXAS!

Those Taggart men—strong, sexy and hard to resist…

You've met Jesse James Taggart in FIREWORKS!
Harlequin Romance #3205 (July 1992)

And Trey Smith—he's THE RED-BLOODED YANKEE!
Harlequin Temptation #413 (October 1992)

Now meet Daniel Boone Taggart in SHOWDOWN!
Harlequin Romance #3242 (January 1993)

And finally the Taggarts who started it all—in LEGEND!
Harlequin Historical #168 (April 1993)

Read all the Taggart romances!
Meet all the Taggart men!

Available wherever Harlequin Books are sold.
